To anyone that has ever chased a dream...

CLOSE SECRETS

JAYNE-LEIGH THOMAS

Published in 2020 by Jayne-Leigh Thomas

© Jayne-Leigh Thomas

Book Design by Lumphanan Press
www.lumphananpress.co.uk

Printed & Bound by Imprint Digital, UK

ISBN: 978-1-8381768-0-8

"Be warned, for what I have to tell you may in due course prove troubling…"

– *Mary King's Close Ghost Story*

PROLOGUE

September, 1639
Royal Mile, Edinburgh, Scotland

Jonet stepped out of the shadowed doorway onto the small street, her wooden pattens squelching in the muck beneath her feet. She wrinkled her nose in disgust at the foul smell which rose up from the ground and shifted the large basket under her arm. Across the narrow street was another doorway, the battered wood covered with a thick layer of human waste from where the muck had been slopped out into the street earlier that morning. Puddles of oily black water lay stagnant along the edges of the Close and bird droppings streaked white across the slick muddy ground. Further down the hill to her right, the Close was beginning to fill with the sounds of people moving up and down the street.

Mrs. Stroud, her small body bent and angular like a broken bird, had already started the early morning busker's call for the tray of spicy parkin and beremeal bannocks which sat steaming on a battered tin plate. Jonet could almost smell the ginger and cinnamon cakes and despite having had breakfast, her stomach rumbled. John Craig was busy hammering nails into the wooden turnpike staircase which lead up to his front door, having to move quickly out of the way as a group of men shouted and raced past, chasing a large sow which had escaped its rope. A new shipment of claret from Bordeaux had arrived the previous afternoon and large crates and barrels of the French red wine were being carted down to Stephen Boyd's wine cellar past the Craig family home. The dark green glass bottles clinked noisily against each other as the old wooden cart bounced down the steep close.

As Jonet stepped forward, a disheveled man brushed past her. Patrick Byrne, one of the city tanners, moved swiftly by, a stack of cut wood hoisted onto his shoulder. Jonet held her breath as he walked by, the stench of horse urine heavy in his wake. Another woman, a maidservant, hurried closely behind him, carrying a stained burlap sack of dirty linens and rags.

Jonet turned quickly and walked out on the Royal Mile. It was just after eight o'clock in the morning and the street was already buzzing with people. Market stalls known as laigh forbooths were being erected on either side of the cobbled street, vendors piling merchandise onto the flimsy wooden tables, the warning shout to a scruffy dog scrambling to keep from being underfoot. The sun blazed unusually hot, especially so early in the morning. The sky was a brilliant azure with clouds like the sweep of a paintbrush over the tall spire of St. Giles Cathedral. The Cathedral during the day was like a grey slumbering beast, but at night the light from the oil lamps brought the great monolith to life, blanketed in shadow and mystery. Today, there was a slight breeze coming from the west that would help with the stench of the city, but with the unexpected warmth, things would quickly ripen in the sun.

To Jonet's left, far off in the distance, a sliver of the sea was visible, the Firth of Forth sparkling in the sunlight. Several large horse-drawn carts were struggling up the street, their heavy loads of vegetables and timber pitching steeply as the wheels bounced over the uneven cobbles. A large group of young men congregated around the Mercat Cross, looking for work. Jonet could not see her brother Alexander among the crowd. The octagonal stone structure loomed over the men and a crow picked lazily at a cluster of dessicated limbs which had been impaled on spikes after last week's hanging. There was a commotion further down the Royal Mile, near Fishmarket Close. Several men squabbled over a crate of fresh oysters that had just been brought up from the sea.

The breeze was like a gentle kiss across her face and slightly ruffled the lace on her bonnet. The Royal Mile was a delight in the summer months. Jonet took a deep breath, content that just for a moment, the stench of the excrement clogging the streets had been replaced by a clean sweetness. Somewhere, bread was being baked and woodsmoke rose from several of the closes. She could hear boistrous shouting and presumed this was from the Star and Garter, one of the most notorious taverns in Edinburgh. Jonet guessed some of the new bottles of French claret must have been opened that morning.

Her mother and sister had left nearly an hour previously to construct their laigh forbooth on the northern side of the Royal Mile before the morning rush of customers. Many of the other stall holders were busy along the northern side of St. Giles Cathedral; the narrow strip of buildings known as the Luckenbooths were opening. Shopkeepers bustled in and out, bringing crates inside, sweeping the entrance, and hanging wooden signs from hooks above the door. Booksellers and stationers chatted with professors from the University, stacks of manuscripts with their colored pigments and gold leaf at their feet. This row of shops sold everything from golf clubs to locks and keys. One shop advertised ladies' shawls, perfumed gloves bordered with silver thread, and frilly petticoats. Another offered soaps, tallow candles, powdered wigs, and tiny stacks of brown paper to burn, combating the smell of the streets.

Jonet walked past the Luckenbooths on the left and the row of low market stalls on her right. Her mother's market stall was further up on the right side, one of the prime locations on the Royal Mile. While it was rare that a woman would be allowed such a prominent position on the Mile, ever since her husband's death, Mary King had been given the rights of a burgess and was held to a higher esteem than most other women in the city. Seconds later Jonet could hear the clear, strong voice of her mother and then there was a flash of yellow. Euphemie. Jonet made a face. Her older sister. Three days ago, Euphemie had received a new frock and had since paraded around in it like a chick preening its feathers. She said it made her look like one of the jonquils growing on the hillside below Edinburgh Castle. Jonet thought she looked like a lump of old butter.

Jonet continued her way through the ever-increasing throngs of people and waited patiently next to the stall. Mary acknowledged her with a nod and a quick smile then went back to discussing the price of a lace ruff with the portly, mustached man that stood at her side. Euphemie was sitting on a wooden stool, her head bent low, adding tiny stitches to an embroidered handkerchief. The needle went in and out of the material slowly; she did not bother to look up.

Their family's low market stall, rented annually from Mr. Failie, was larger than most on the Mile. A wooden table set on sturdy legs with a thin expanse of cloth stretched over the top of the stall to provide protection from the sun and the rain. On the surface of the table, examples of Mary's fine needlework were arranged in rows. Tablecloths, table runners, handkerchiefs, and curtains were stacked on one side with finer clothes, detailed with tiny birds and flowers, on the other. Mary's exquisite embroidery was in high demand among the wealthy in Edinburgh and she did the majority of the detailed sewing, leaving the simpler tasks like mending seams and attaching buttons to her daughters. Within the pile of pillowcases, Jonet could see a corner of dark red fabric and recognized it as the piece she had completed the night before. The portly man had lumbered away, carrying two parcels of embroidered linen with him. Mary turned to her youngest daughter, a smile on her face.

"Good morning Jonet." Mary reached out and straightened her daughter's bonnet. Although nearly reaching her 35th year, she was still an attractive woman, dressed in pale blue dress with dark stitching, a red stomacher secured tightly around her middle. Her skirts were full and voluminous with tiny roses embroidered at the hem. The silver Luckenbooth brooch, which had been a gift from her late husband Thomas Nimmo on their betrothal, was fastened on her chest and flashed in the sunlight as she moved.

"Good morning Mother."

"You remember everything that I asked you to pick up this morning?"

"Aye, I did. I hope this will carry it all." Jonet held up the large basket for her mother to see. Mary nodded approvingly.

"Yes, that should be fine. Had Anne started on the washing when you left?" Anne was their housemaid.

"Yes'm. I think so. She said she would start on the bedclothes first but would need to fetch a watercarrier to bring some water up from the Loch." Again Mary nodded.

"Now run along my dear. It is likely to be quite warm again today and I don't want the cheese to spoil before you get it home. And you can start attaching a new length of lace to one of the white blouses I left in the cedar chest when you return."

Jonet nodded then turned up the Royal Mile to the Lawnmarket. It was busier this time of year, with the additional fruits and vegetables growing in the lands surrounding Edinburgh. Jonet had heard whispered stories of famine in the north, people reduced to eating dogs and seaweed to survive, but luckily, Edinburgh had yet to fall on those hard times as the summer fruits were already abundantly plentiful. She could see the large crowds ahead, men stacking crates of vegetables alongside the street, women arranging linens and baskets of eggs on the stall fronts, hungry dogs winding their way in between the stalls. Most folk would be making their way to the Butter Tron at the head of the West Bow. The West Bow was the western entrance to the city and horse-drawn carts were trudging steadily up the hill from the Grassmarket, past the open gates. Several carts had already pulled up alongside the small stone building that had been erected in the middle of the street at the western end of the Lawnmarket. Large queues of merchants holding bundles of cheese and butter were winding their way to its entrance, anxious to have their merchandise weighed, so that business could begin. Outside the front of Thomas Gladstone's tenement building, there was a chorus of snuffling and grunting from the trio of black and white pigs, anxious for any scraps of food dropped or thrown their way.

Thomas was outside the building, standing hands on hips, giving directions to several men who were adding the finishing touches to the new painted ceiling within his home. Renovations to this building had first started in 1617 and work was constantly being done. The painters trudged up the turnpike stair at the front of the building, arms laden with wooden ladders, brushes, and small tins of paint in colors of ochre, white, and black. Thomas's wife stood underneath the grand arcade front, discussing the price of linen with Lady Geida Smith, wife of Sir Walter Grey. Sir Walter himself stood further down the Lawnmarket at the entrance of Wardrop's Close and from one of the narrow streets, there was the wheezing whine and squeal of a bagpipe.

Jonet stood at the entrance of the market and took a satisfying breath. Being the eldest, Euphemie normally had the job of going to the markets each morning, but as she spent more time helping Mary at their stall and her two brothers were busy with their apprenticeships, the job of running errands had fallen to Jonet. Not that she minded. There was something exciting about the busy atmosphere, the smell of fresh fruit, the small posies of brightly colored wildflowers, and the chance to get out of the house to see the exotic new goods piled high in the stalls, recently brought up off the ships at Leith Harbor. Especially as the remaining hours of the day she was stuck inside, helping Anne in the house, sewing, or reading.

Up one side of the Lawnmarket, stalls were piled high with rows of hard green Bramley apples, small punnets of woodland strawberries, and shiny gooseberries, the pale green globes with their taut, veiny skins. Clumps of dusty brown potatoes, thick bunches of fat hen tied with twine, and bundles of leeks were arranged neatly on the stalls. Women walked up and down the rows between the stalls with ceramic jars of fresh milk. Lumps of wet cheese wrapped in cloth sat next to twisted grey mushrooms and bundles of peat and firewood were stacked haphazardly against the stall legs. Jonet went from one stall to another, gathering the goods her mother had requested and carefully counting the silver coins before handing them off to the merchant.

Although not on the list, Jonet stopped and gazed longingly at the summer strawberries, the tiny heart-shaped fruit glossy and red under the sun. Mrs. Bridle, a regular customer of her mother's, noticed her gaze and kindly offered her one to sample. Jonet lifted it to her nose and breathed in the delightful smell, then popped it into her mouth. A rush of sweetness raced over her tongue.

Basket heaving, Jonet turned and wound her way back through the pressing crowd to the stalls near the Tolbooth. Here, the goods were exotic and more luxurious, the clientele more refined than that up in the Lawnmarket. Merchants proudly displayed French clocks, Turkish rugs, spindle whorls of elephant ivory, and expensive foodstuffs such as pepper, bags of currants, bunches of garlic, figs, anchovies, capers, and jars of pickles and hard green olives. Wooden furniture was arranged in corners of the market square. Jonet took her time, walking from stall to stall, pausing at one booth near the Tolbooth where men attempted to construct a feather bed in the middle of the street. On the western platform extending from the Tolbooth, two men were making repairs to the Maiden. Although another execution wasn't scheduled for four days, the blade was being sharpened, a new rope attached, and the sounds from their tools echoed across the busy square.

On the southern side of St. Giles Cathedral, the elite of the city perused the stalls set out by the gold and silversmiths. Ladies glistened in silks and damask shoes and men in velvet lined jackets with lace collars and embroidered hose walked amongst each other, chatting in low cadences, occasionally lifting a piece to the light. Silver candlesticks and stout tappit hens were set out on swatches of fine linen and jewelry was displayed decadently on squares of black velvet. Intricate Luckenbooth brooches, gold signet rings, and glossy pearl earrings winked in the morning sunlight. Ropes of ornate gold chain lie nestled against emerald pendants. Jonet saw her family's landlord, Mr. Bannantyne, leaning low to examine a pair of mother-of-pearl cufflinks, his curled grey wig slipping low on his brow.

The sun was starting to burn high in the sky over the Cathedral. Jonet remembered her mother's warning not to let the cheese spoil, and turned for home, stopping only momentarily to peek down into the Krames, the dark, narrow passage between the Cathedral and the Luckenbooths. This street, filled with children's toys like wooden puppets, rag dolls, marbles, and bone animal carvings at Christmas, contained a menagerie of goods and merchants during the rest of the year. Scissor and knife grinders stood side by side with candy men and people selling horn cups, pewter silverware, bags of salt, and paper lanterns.

Jonet was startled to hear a loud commotion behind her. Turning, she gasped in fear as a horse drawn cart bolted its way up the High Street, the large Breton horse at the front wild and frightened. The owner, whose girth was almost as much as his height, bellowed and tried to run after the runaway horse as turnips, parsnips, and leafy cabbages flew from the back of the rickety cart. The wheels twisted sharply in the ruts between the uneven, cracked cobbles, and there was a large crack as the rear axle snapped, sending the cart teetering onto its left side and pulling the horse to a skidding stop. Jonet moved back quickly out of the way but fell with a small cry of pain as her ankle twisted on one of the loose cobbles.

Mr. Gowrie, his bald head red and glistening with sweat, lumbered up to his startled horse, mumbling something about 'damned bees'. The horse, its ears flat to its head, eyes rolling, foam falling from its mouth, pranced and stomped its hooves in agitation. With the wagon lay on its side, young boys frantically chased after the turnips which were rolling across the stones down the street. Anxious to be out of the way, Jonet lifted herself quickly up and hobbled over to a small wooden bench next to the Cathedral. Her skirts were now stained from the muck in the street and her ankle was starting to throb. She reached down and gingerly massaged her stockinged foot, watching as the cart was turned up right and the remaining vegetables were loaded back into the wagon.

She glanced down and noticed in dismay that the cheese she had bought had fallen out of the basket and so had several of the potatoes, their golden skins now flecked with mud. She quickly gathered them back into the basket and tried to nudge the dislodged cobble back into place with her good foot. Almost fixed. With a defiant stomp, Jonet crushed the stone back into the ground. There was a large crunching sound as the stone was forced back into place.

Jonet frowned at the strange sound. It hadn't sounded like stone on stone but rather stone on *metal*. She set the basket down and reached her fingers into the cracks between the stones. Stomping on the stone hadn't lodged it back into place and it was easy to remove. Wet black earth gathered under her nails as she scraped away at the ground to reveal something nestled into the corner of the empty space.

It was a knotted chain, thickly coated in mud and grime. She wrapped the chain around her fingers and gave a slight tug. With a soft sucking sound, the chain was set free. There was a hard stone attached to the end of the chain and rubbing at it with her thumb, Jonet was rewarded with a flash of color. Her heart skipped a beat. *Gold.* Perhaps it was something that one of the goldsmiths had dropped on their way to the market. She shoved the street cobble back into the rectangular space and making a pretense of dusting off her dress, slipped the chain into the folds of her skirt. Keeping her head down, she hurried through the throngs of people on the Royal Mile to the turn-pike stair which lead up to her house. Taking one last furtive glance around, Jonet pushed through the door and entered the kitchen. She held her breath. Silence. Good. Anne was still out attending to the washing. She dropped the basket onto the small table next to the fireplace and went through to the main chamber. Her mother's beautifully carved bed dominated one corner of the room but Jonet passed quickly to the secretaire where there was a white ceramic bowl and ewer on a stand next to the window. With shaking hands, she poured a small amount of water from the ewer into the bottom of the bowl and dropped the chain into it. The water turned brown, muddy swirls darkening the bowl, and after swishing the chain through the water several times, Jonet lifted it, dripping up to the light.

The sunlight coming through the cloudy pane of glass caught the amethyst stone on the end of the chain, sending a shaft of lavender across the room. Three colored jewels were set into a delicate gold crown above the heart-shaped stone and they sparkled as the chain twirled. Jonet patted it dry with a piece of muslin cloth and went to sit on a chair next to the window ledge.

It was a necklace. The clasp at one end was bent slightly,

clearly broken. It would be easy for someone to lose something valuable, the streets swallowing up dropped or discarded objects into the piles of mud and filth which poured out from the closes. She sat for a long while, mesmerized by the beauty and elegance of the piece and marveling at the colored beams of light which danced around the room. She could envision herself wearing something as grand a piece as this, perhaps at one of Edinburgh's balls or on her wedding day. But then fear gnawed at her day-dreaming. She wouldn't be permitted to keep it. Her mother would demand to know where she got it and would try and locate its owner. Euphemie would want to wear it and heavens only knew what would happen if Anne knew. She might even try to steal it. Her stomach turned as she realized it wouldn't be long before Anne would be back to the house, anxious to continue with the household chores and prepare the evening meal.

Jonet made a decision. She would somehow keep the necklace. Since it had been *beneath* the stone, she reckoned that it had been there a while and surely whomever had lost it would have given up looking for it by now. But she would have to hide it, somewhere safe until she could decide what to do with it. Or find out more about it. Perhaps the owner had been a wealthy lady, so wealthy, that a lost necklace wouldn't mean much to her and that Jonet would be allowed to keep it. But until then, it must remain hidden away. Jonet smiled. She had the perfect idea.

*   *   *

That evening after supper, Jonet sat by the light of a beeswax candle, adding tiny stitches to a silk handkerchief. The location she had selected for the necklace wasn't ideal; it was currently nestled in behind a satchel of cloves within the spice cabinet, but it would suffice until she could move it to a more secure location. She had the location already in mind and in a few days' time, when she was alone, she would move the necklace. She smiled to herself. She must write about today in her diary. She could imagine the entry in her mind as she sewed…

September 8, 1639

Today was the most exciting of days. I found a necklace on the Royal Mile and it is the most beautiful thing I have ever seen. Although I should endeavor to locate its owner, my desire to keep it is overwhelmingly strong and I have decided to hide it away, where no one will find it. I have decided to put it in the most peculiar of places, somewhere no one would ever imagine…

1

S unlight flits in between the fast moving clouds racing across a flawless Edinburgh sky. Hundreds of tourists are milling up and down the Royal Mile, perusing the vendors' stalls on either side of the cobbled street. These vendors are selling felt hats, cloth bags, tooled leather, and jewelry made of pale green Highland marble. It is a reminiscent scene, back to the days of the city's famous Luckenbooths. A large group of Spanish tourists gather beneath the Mercat Cross, the gilded unicorn at the top glinting in the pale autumn light. A bagpipe wheezes from somewhere up in the Lawnmarket and several children jump around the stone Heart of Midlothian next to St. Giles cathedral. Across from the cathedral on the northern side, there is a narrow, covered passage called Warriston's Close which slopes downwards off the High Street. Three tour guides, in 17th century costume, stand chatting with passersby and handing out leaflets. They are advertising The Real Mary King's Close, which is a mere 30 meters behind them.

Warriston's Close is flanked on either side with clusters of black and white balloons and there is a large sign pointing visitors down the passage and into an ornate black wrought iron gate. Behind the gate is a small courtyard surrounded by a wall of green foliage and white fairy lights. It is quaint and gives an understated feeling of a medieval garden. Silver pots overflow with various herbs; geraniums, lobelia, and purple Scottish heather. Tables and chairs are arranged under a large parasol; black metal lanterns with flickering candles sit next to menus on the table tops. The smell of rich coffee and hot soup wafts through the air and there is the gentle whirring sound of machinery as coffee beans are ground in the café and the steam wand lets off a blasting hiss. On the CD player, Runrig sing gaily about the bonny banks of Loch Lomond. Glossy cakes are arranged next to a row of flavored syrups and a freezer of Mackie's ice cream. Small trees in a long wicker planter frame a large sign which explains the café's location in relation to where the Royal Exchange Coffee House stood during its prominent years in the 18th century.

The entrance to The Real Mary King's Close is through the large wooden door and into the gift shop. This historic site is the only 5-star underground attraction in the city. Opened in 2003, it provides guests with the rare opportunity to experience the streets and houses preserved beneath the City Chambers building, formerly the Royal Exchange of 1753. There are guided tours leaving the gift shop every 15 minutes which last for one hour. I am one of these tour guides.

I play Jonet Nimmo, the daughter of Mary King, who was born in 1622. One of four children, Jonet lived in Edinburgh until she married, moving to her husband's manor house four days after her seventeenth birthday.

I stand in the doorway leading down into the Close, ushering people out of the darkness and into the gift shop for the end of their tour. With a sigh of relief, I shut the door when they have all gone. I quickly untie my bonnet and have the laces nearly undone in my corset by the time I reach the changing room. Less than five minutes later, I am inconspicuous to the crowds in jeans and a jumper and slip out the front entrance, waving to Eilidh in the café as I go.

Out on the High Street I take a cleansing breath. A long day of four tours, Italian school children, a forever failing torch, and a broken shoelace. I am ready to go home.

The sun is starting to slip in the west, edging behind Edinburgh Castle, but the Cathedral still glows with an ethereal golden light. It is nearly half past six. The market stalls along the High Street are being taken down and most of the street performers have either left or are packing their bags and counting the coins in their tins. Most of the shops have closed, but behind me in the Close, tours will run until 10 pm.

I started working at Mary King's Close a little over a year ago and are now considered to be one of the 'veterans'. It's a job where people, mainly students, stay on as temporary staff for a couple months during the summer or stay on permanently and try to make a living on a tour guide salary. I'm in both camps. I am currently studying for a PhD in history at the University of Edinburgh and although I have been lucky enough to obtain a scholarship, an extra few pounds each month helps to make sure the bills are paid.

Home is luckily a five minute walk from the Close. Past St. Giles Cathedral heading west, up the Lawnmarket, along Johnston's Terrace, and then down Patrick Geddes' steps and Castle Wynd to a flat just off the Grassmarket. Formerly a medieval market and place for public executions, the Grassmarket is a rectangular area which now thrives with cafes, pubs, restaurants, and shops. Prior to being used as a marketplace, it was a grassy area for open air theatre and royal jousting during the 12th and 13th centuries. I love the imagery of colored banners, the bunting, and flags fluttering in the breeze, crowds lined up at the expanse of the tournament field. The thick clouds from the horses' nostrils mingling with the early morning mist that settles over the grass; the horses pawing anxiously at the wet turf, the clank of armor, and the mixed cries of delight and disappointment when riders were unseated.

Above the field on the hillside, were the lush orchards and gardens of Edinburgh Castle. Today the former gardens are a part of King's Stables Road, where horses were kept below the castle. It has recently been transformed into a small park next to Granny's Green Steps, with bench seating around feathery lavender plants. The whole area has become the stomping grounds for tiny fawn colored rabbits that hide away in the brush above the road.

My flat is small but adequate with a private garden and a wonderful view of the Castle from the kitchen and living room windows. I let myself in the door and am hit by a blast of warm air, the smells of meat and onions heavy. My flatmate David has recently started dating French-born Therese and is keen to take any opportunity to impress. David is also a PhD student in my department, studying the Roman occupation of Rough Castle Fort near Falkirk. We have lived together for over two years and although his tidiness in the bathroom leaves something to be desired, we get along well.

Fifteen minutes later I am showered and starving. I enter the living room where David and Therese are cuddled up on the couch with a bottle of Cabernet Sauvignon. *Chocolat* flickers from the flat screen monitor perched on the TV stand.

I give them a small hello and try and throw something together quickly for dinner so I am out of their way.

Cooking is not my forte. Most of my meals consist of yogurt, fruit, and cold sausage rolls. Tonight I scrounge around and come up with three sliced tomatoes, a ball of low fat mozzarella, and two microwaved vegetarian sausages. Sufficient.

I eat dinner in my room and check my emails. Two messages from Dad updating me on the weather and fishing conditions at the nearby river back home, one from Orange UK stating my phone bill is overdue, and two Facebook notices that something I posted last night has been 'liked'. Nothing overly interesting or urgent then. I finish and lay the plate on the floor then lean back against the headboard of my bed, closing my eyes for a moment's rest. I have just finished a seven hour shift, but there is little time before I'll be back to work.

* * *

Across the country, a man sits down in the large upholstered armchair next to the fireplace and downs a crystal glass full of Glenmorangie. He pours another measure and sits musing. He is large, muscled, ex-military, his movements sharp and precise. His study is paneled in dark wood with old furniture and although the curtains are drawn, he can hear the soft patter of rain on the windows. Throughout the room, surfaces are piled high with papers. Photocopies, maps, drawings, and blueprints are covered with penciled notes and highlighted sections. The main table in the room is also covered with books, pens, cotton gloves, a magnifying glass, tweezers, and a used tea mug. There is a grandfather clock in one corner dating from 1705 and it still ticks faithfully. A small tape recorder lies on the small table next to him and he looks at it in disgust. To avoid it, he picks up the bronze poker and stabs at the logs in the fire. Small golden sparks leap from the wood and the fire starts to blaze. He is starting to hate this endeavor but then realizes with a stab of guilt of his selfishness and with a sigh, picks up the recorder. He is about halfway through; he has already listened to it twice. It's about committing things to memory and so he settles back into the chair, nurses the Glenmorangie for a moment, then pushes play.

"This is what we call our 17th century house and it has been here for 400 years. It was a middle class house with this room being the kitchen. The original grinding stone…"

The voice that fills the room is lilting, softly accented. It is a storyteller's voice, descriptive, expressive, and brings the audience's imagination to life. It is high pitched and full of emotion one moment, then drops to a silvery whisper the next, commanding attention and luring the listener in. It is also a stage voice, her dulcet tones dramatic, vivid, and melodious. Despite her honeyed tones, it is not her voice he is interested in.

There is a hardwood gun case on the table near his elbow. It is made of stained Scottish oak with a small brass latch on the front. The inside is lined with faded red felt and it holds his grandfather's service weapon from WWII, a semi-automatic, Browning Hi-Power 9mm. A bottle of gun solvent, a wire brush, and an oily rag sit next to it. *To Colin, Love Grandpa.* This gun is the only thing he has left of his grandfather's. He picks up the gun from the case, turning it over in his hands. It has been several years since he has taken it out of its case and it is in need of a good clean. He is not even certain if it will still fire. The blued steel is worn and scratched and the checkering on the wood grip has been worn smooth from years of handling. His finger curves with familiarity over the trigger. He hasn't handled a gun since four years ago in Afghanistan; he is in no hurry to handle one now.

The voice from the tape recorder has moved on and is now discussing window tax. She is getting close to where he needs her to be.

2

It is dark when I leave the flat. My shoes squelch up Candlemaker Row as I make my way to my second job. And to me, the most important.

I swipe my University card through the security system on the panel next to the door and enter my code. The panel beeps with a bright green light as I am granted clearance and there is a soft sucking noise as the lock releases. The atrium is dark but as soon as I step in, the lights flicker to life overhead. At my feet lies a large University of Edinburgh doormat with the logo in bright blue, red, and white. Postgraduate students working in the department after hours are required to check-in with security upon their arrival and departure. I walk to the phone hanging on the wall.

"Security. Frank speaking."

"Hi Frank. It's Carole in History. Just checking in."

"21:04 arrival. Phone when you leave." He hangs up, presumably in a hurry to get back to the fish and chip supper which is his nightly meal and makes the building smell of grease and vinegar.

My lab is located on the second floor of the History department. History had originally been located near the

Old High School Yards building off of Infirmary Street, but departmental shuffling put us nearer to Bristo Square and the old medical buildings. An architectural table takes up the majority of the small space, a magnifying glass/lamp combination stretches like a probing eye above the worktop. A side bench is overloaded with a small umbrella tree plant, a kettle, three coffee cups, and a jar of instant Columbian. I share my office with a woman from archaeology who is researching Bell Beakers from the Mediterranean, but for the moment is on an excavation trip overseas, so I am blissfully left to work alone for nearly 3 months.

Specializing in paleography, the study of ancient handwriting, my research is a spin-off from the work I completed for my Master's thesis. Having spent months learning how to transcribe dozens of medieval Scottish manuscripts and historical texts, I was given the opportunity to work with a series of 17th century letters known as the Nimmo letters. These letters, written by Jonet Nimmo to her brother Alexander during the middle of the 17th century, had been hidden away in a small whalebone casket until their re-discovery in 2001.

The Nimmo letters were first discovered in 1876 by a member of the Stuart-Whyte family. They remained a secret family heirloom until being publicly revealed by the matriarch of the family, Vivienne Stuart-Whyte. A direct descendant of Alexander Nimmo, Vivienne is a well-known philanthropist in Edinburgh, a woman with too much time, too much money, and who wears her makeup like a circus clown. The letters were donated to the National Museum in an elaborate, press-filled ceremony, with Vivienne sashaying through her audience in a cloud of Chanel No. 5, her sagging neck choked with meters of white pearls.

The Nimmo letters are brought to the University a few sheets at a time by one of the museum couriers; I am close to completing them. There is only one more set to be brought over from the National Museum of Scotland. The letter in front of me is from 1641.

I slip on a pair of cotton gloves and adjust the light over the fragile page. Like the others, the letter was written on a wrinkled yellow page, the black ink faded to brown over the years. Jonet's writing is fluid, but spidery and she is remarkably educated for someone from the 17th century. There is something in the corner, a dark stain, and although it may be an ink splotch, it looks more like a smear of blood. Perhaps a papercut. These letters speak volumes to me, not just about Jonet's life but the life of those around her, fellow citizens of Scotland during the 17th century, and I am fiercely possessive of them. A couple of weeks ago, I realized that small smudges of ink had been from teardrops; Jonet's tears as she wrote of the death of her mother in 1644. I cried with her.

Four days after her marriage, Jonet left Edinburgh and moved into her new family's manor house out in the Scottish countryside. An arranged marriage, Jonet's relationship with Lord Sinclair was full of love and adoration, although she only lived to a mere 33 years, dying in 1655. She was seventeen at the time of the marriage.

Dearest Alexander,

I write to you with the highest hopes that you and your family are well. Sometime has passed since your last letter and I am hoping that you are happily busy as a new husband and father and that you have not forgotten your youngest sister...

When I look up at the clock again, it is 12:15 am. I have drained two cups of coffee and one Diet Coke sits half empty on the counter. My eyes ache and burn from looking through the magnifying glass for so long. I should head home; I have work at the Close tomorrow. A 10:30 am start, which will allow me some decent sleep. I place the letter carefully back into its protective cover then slip it into a locked cabinet on the far side of the room. I sleep better knowing Jonet's letters are locked away.

3

olin pushed through the heavy oak doors, shifting his pack slightly as he squeezes past a group of elderly Japanese women clucking over a map of the city. As with previous visits, the gift shop was busy, people standing in queues to purchase postcards, guide books, and other Scottish memorabilia. He glanced at his watch. Still several minutes to go. Things would start predictably with a heavy brass bell being rung, the tour announced, and then the tour group would file in like a herd of cattle to meet their guide. There was no need to check-in so he went to the back of the shop to make a pretense of perusing through the selection of books. The shelves were filled with books on paranormal activity, a series of first-hand accounts of 'ghostly' encounters, and Scottish history. Behind him at the main desk, the staff were swamped with phones ringing, photos being printed, and bookings being made for future tours. Above Colin's head a security camera whirled, recording his every move; he wasn't concerned.

He lingered in front of the plastic scale model of the Close, lost in his own troubled thoughts when something bumped his elbow. Or someone. A short fat woman with peroxide blond hair jostled in next to him, peering at the model and poking her fat sausage-like fingers at the small plastic buildings. He looked down at her in disgust. The smell of garlic and body odor radiated from her body in waves and rolls of fat were squeezed into a tight shirt. Oblivious to his obvious disgust, she leaned in and leered towards him, revealing a row of nicotine-stained teeth. Something brown was lodged in between her top incisors. He turned away just as she said loudly, "Can you believe people were bricked in and lived underground?"

"For god's sake," Colin muttered under his breath, his stomach roiling from the smell coming out from her mouth. Fools. Most tourists didn't give a damn about history. Traveling had become about being herded like a farm animal from one money-sucking attraction to another and spending money on worthless dust-catching rubbish. He glanced again at his watch. Bang on 2:00 pm. An anorexic looking brunette with a bad dye job held the bell in one hand and a clipboard in another.

"Good afternoon ladies and gentlemen and welcome to the Real Mary King's Close. Now is the start of the 2 o'clock tour. If you do have a booking, please make your way to me and state the name you booked under."

The fat woman scurried away to join her husband but Colin's relief was short-lived as he realized she would be on the tour with him.

"Name sir?" The woman's name badge read Eilidh. She didn't even look up at him, her pen running over the names on the list.

"Wilson." He stated, staring straight ahead. Not his real surname, but generic. Forgettable. He was nearly through the door when her voice startled him.

"Would you like me to have your bag placed into one of our

security lockers for the duration of the tour?" Her voice was nasal and whiny.

"No thank you." Colin said gruffly and shuffled himself into the back of the room. There were 19 of them in total, squeezed in between a gauzy wall hanging and a waist-high partition capped with a wooden banister. He took a deep breath, said a small prayer to retain his sanity, and waited for the tour to begin.

4

I walk out of the gift shop and behind the sign that says 'Staff Only'. The staff room door has a large set of buttons above the handle and I punch the code in. I am greeted by the smell of burnt curry and fish upon entering the room. Oliver is sitting at the computer with a microwavable curry meal, checking football scores. I have no idea where the fish smell is coming from. I only have a twenty minute break before my next tour, so I grab a glass of water and sit down at the small table we crowd around during lunch. There is only a minute or two of peace, the sole sounds being from Oliver sporadically tapping the keyboard and the hum of the server which sits in the corner of the room. Then a number is swiftly punched into the lock and the door flies open, nearly knocking Oliver's curry from his hand. He doesn't notice. Liverpool won last night and Oliver is a die-hard Manchester United fan. He is taking the loss hard. He could have been knocked out of the chair and probably wouldn't have noticed.

The woman who opened the door moves like a force of nature through the room, loud and often destructive. Jolyne is our resident American tour guide and she is not only accident prone but has a tendency to break most of the dishes and/or appliances in the staff room. She accidentally tore the hinge out of the staff room door several days prior.

"Hot damn!" She says exasperated and sits down with a swirl of purple satin on the couch. Her lace bonnet goes flying as she tears it off her head and throws it down on the cushion beside her. Jolyne is from somewhere in the American West, Utah, Nevada, or Arizona, although I can never remember which. She is stereotypically American; lives on a horse ranch, owns several guns, and will salute as her way of saying goodbye. She too is studying for her PhD at the University of Edinburgh, focusing on paranormal psychology. Also like myself, she plays Jonet Nimmo, although she has developed a ridiculous faux-British voice for her tours to hide her accent. She is jokingly under orders from the management to not consume more than one cup of coffee before or during her work shift. Otherwise, she will go into hurricane mode and management is only half-joking.

"Bad tour?" I ask. Jolyne was hired at the same time I was and she is one of my favorite people to work with at the Close.

She snorts sarcastically and rolls her eyes and for a moment I think she will sit there and try and relax but I am quickly proven wrong. She never sits still for long.

"DAMN. I stink. Like an old cow." She says, smelling the sleeve of her lacy white blouse. Jumping up and grabbing the can of air freshener off the counter, she stomps towards the door. Oliver is still obsessing over the football, oblivious to both us and the rapidly cooling curry congealing in the bottom of the plastic tray. Jolyne flings the door open and blasts her costume down with the lavender scented spray, then gives her armpits a quick blast before coming back in the room.

"Any better?"

I try hard not to laugh. "I couldn't smell you before but now you smell like the toilets. Or an old lady's house."

She grins at me. "Hmm. I might have over done it. Where's my coffee?" She shouts, turning on her heel and striding towards the server and starts rummaging through the pile of papers and bags on the top.

"Is Owen still monitoring your caffeine intake?" I ask. Owen is our general manager.

"Yep. They say I can have one cup a day while I'm at work. But what the management doesn't know is that I take three shots of espresso in that ONE cup." She chuckles at her secret deception, and then lets out a loud shout of success. She holds up her paper coffee cup over her head, triumph for having found it, but the lid flies off and coffee streams down the cup, over her hand, and onto her skirt.

"Aw heck!" She shouts again, flinging the cup down and reaching for the tea towel draped over the radiator by the window. Her elbow hits the dish rack and it slides sideways, sending a plate and two coffee cups crashing loudly into the sink.

The door opens again and Lorna comes in. Lorna is one of our managers, in charge of the café and the gift shop. She has a glimmer of amusement in her eyes and she is trying not to smile. She looks like the cat that ate the canary. She is looking right at me.

"Well, it appears you have a fan or two." She says and I notice that she is carrying a small bag and an envelope.

"Secret admirer! Woop!" Jolyne shouts from the sink. "Or maybe some creepy stalker! There is another crash as the container holding the cutlery is tipped over. Swearing ensues.

"What is it?" I ask and Lorna hands me both items.

"Have a look. The bag came in this morning from a German guy and I'm not sure when the letter arrived. Might have been yesterday."

I set the envelope down and open the bag. It is a plastic bag from one of the tourist shops on the Royal Mile and contains a small stuffed sheep with a red bow around its neck. There is no note, no explanation. I feel my face blushing and I hold it up. Jolyne and Lorna are laughing. "Did the German guy say anything?"

"He told April at the front desk to make sure that it got to the Jonet in the green dress. He didn't want to leave a name or a note, just asked that you get this. He was on your tour yesterday."

I think back and vaguely remember a German man on my morning tour yesterday, how I had helped him with his audio guide and given him a map of the city. Lorna shrugs and smiles, then walks out. Oliver follows her, going to start his tour and it won't be long before someone else just coming up off a tour joins us. Jolyne is still at the sink, in the process of soaking her satin skirt, cursing under her breath. She is muttering about hoping it will be dry before her next tour, but I tune her out and turn to the envelope on the table. I have never gotten gifts like this from tourists before. Tips, cups of coffee, throat lozenges, flag pins, and tissues, yes. Actual presents, no.

I use a pen lying on the table to peel the flap of the envelope back. The sheet of paper I take out is stiff and precisely folded and when I open it, my stomach flips.

It is a photocopy of a document. The copied handwriting is angled and written in cursive. But I know this writing like the back of my hand, would recognize it anywhere, having spent hours upon hours studying it. It is Jonet Nimmo's handwriting and after quickly glancing over it, I know that it is not from one of the letters I have studied for my PhD. This is something else. But from where?

There is nothing else with the copied page. No note, no additional handwriting, no address. Just my name printed in black ink on the front. A shiver goes down my back as I realize that the person that left this for me knows who I am and obviously knows of my research. Perhaps one of my colleagues playing a joke? But surely not. There are few people with access to the Nimmo letters and again, this isn't something from that collection.

I quickly fold the letter back up and shove it back in the envelope. Jolyne has abandoned her quest to drown her skirt and is at the counter with her back to me, pushing all the buttons on the microwave at once, trying to heat up her lunch. I leave her to cooking her soup on the popcorn mode and hide the letter in the satin pouch that hangs from my waist. I push my way through the gift shop and go down to the changing room. It is the one place I think of that I might be able to look over the letter without anyone asking me about it.

The changing room is blissfully silent after the hordes of people and children in the gift shop. I sit down on one of the chairs and take the letter back out again. No question, it is Jonet's handwriting, but this is definitely not something I have ever seen. Some of the words are squeezed together, extremely slanted as if written in a hurry, and I know it is going to take some time to try and decipher all the words. I unlock my locker and place the envelope on the top shelf, and then with a sigh, head back up to the gift shop. It is tour time.

5

The walls were painted black and it was dark, with small overhead spotlights illuminating the Real Mary King's Close sign and the large blown-up print of Edinburgh from 1647. There were murmurs and whispers of excitement as the door to the small room was closed and suddenly *she* appeared out of the darkness. Several people gasped as she came fully into view, blond hair the color of corn silk falling to her waist and shimmering under the lights in a satin dress of pale green. She was a pretty woman, and in another life Colin might have been complementary of her looks, but there were other things on his mind. And he had seen her before on other tours so the staged effect of a flaxen-haired siren arising from the shadowy depths had lost its allure at least four tours ago.

"Good afternoon and welcome to the Real Mary King's Close. My name is Jonet Nimmo and I was one of Mary King's daughters." Her voice washed over him like a balm, having become so familiar to him after hours of late night sessions next to the fire with the tape recorder. It was soft, alluring, almost seductive even, and he watched as people grew silent and leaned forward, straining to catch every word that fell from her lips. He knew this wasn't her real voice, simply a staged accent but nevertheless it did the trick. The tourists were hooked.

The smells of old dust and stagnant air filled his nostrils as they descended into the bowels of the Close. Settling into the back of the group with the yawning chasm of the ancient street behind him, he ran through the layout of the site in his head. Next would be the laigh house where she would pretend to throw the toilet contents out onto the street, eliciting groans and sighs of disgust as she described the filth people would have lived in. Then on to the murder room, where wax figurines stood in an eternal pose of horror and discovery, through several more vaulted rooms, then finally, the fun would begin.

6

I show the German couple on audio guides the number 7 painted on a wooden block on the door to Pearson's Close, then push through into the shadowed, gloomy darkness of the narrow passage. The air here is cooler; the orange beams from the lanterns and fake candles flicker over the stone walls and send shafts of light into the dark recesses. Pearson's is quiet, save for the soft shuffling of people following behind me. I stop halfway down the close. There is no one in the 17th century house to my right and there are no voices echoing up from the spiral staircase ahead. Greg's group, having started their tour 15 minutes in front of me, should be in the 17th century house. This means that Erica's group is 30 minutes ahead, either still in the main Close or getting ready to go back up to the top. Greg's group earlier sounded rowdy, with screams of genuine fear when he squeaked the rat at them in the plague room. But they are nowhere to be seen. Then there is a rushing sound and I realize that Greg's group is still in listening to the ghost story. He is running behind schedule and it will mean that I will need to slow down or risk our two groups running into each other later in the tour.

I push open the door to the cowshed. The smell hits me

like a wave and the air is hot, stale, and lifeless. There is a soft lowing emanating from the soundtrack, the speakers hidden cleverly in the long rectangular trough set against the left wall. I stand patiently, holding the door open for my group which is still slowly ambling down Pearson's Close.

They aren't a bad bunch. I've definitely had worse. A full twenty, with the German couple on audio guides who seem bewildered at the experience, but are quietly following along; a man who insists on jangling the coins in his pocket while I'm talking; another man, his face mottled and veiny like that of a heavy drinker, his jaws slapping together as his gum is devoured, jowls jiggling dangerously as saliva is sucked back into between his teeth; and a large American woman that keeps asking questions before I have the chance to give an explanation of the room or the objects within them. I hate this. I never object to people asking questions, in fact I gratefully welcome them, as it gives a break from the repetition of the tours and lets me know who is interested and paying attention. But it wears me down when people immediately ask a question rather than letting me give the explanation first. Especially when it is the same person. *Especially* when they do this more than once. There is also a large man that stays near the back of the group with a large pack. He has a Celtic knot symbol shaved into the back of his head and is wearing neon orange camouflage pants with army boots. He seems slightly distracted and I am not sure if this is because perhaps his English isn't very good and he is having trouble following along. But for the most part, the tour is fine.

I pay close attention to the people on my tour. Preemptive damage control you might say. This allows me to know as soon as possible if people are struggling with the language, becoming irritated for whatever reason, or perhaps feeling a bit unwell. It also allows me to make sure that if for some reason I acquire a tourist from another tour, I can recognize them and get them back to the correct group. While you wouldn't think this would generally be a problem, unfortunately people wander off on their own in the Close, especially the foreigners who lag behind and get disoriented and end up tagging onto someone else's tour.

Today the cowshed smells stronger than usual. Even stronger than it was this morning. As my group shuffles in, there are the predictable cries of disgust and people covering their mouths as they file in onto the flat stone slabs to the right. I watch for the German couple, making sure they have seen the number 8 sign for their audio guide and that they do not venture too far away from the group. Once they are all in the room, I continue.

I explain why cows were kept within the city walls and show the group the dookit holes in the walls where the cows would have be tethered for milking. I point out to them the cobblestones which would have aided in cleanup and the narrow canal in the stone floor where the blood would have run before being collected for Scots black pudding. There are again several squeals of disgust, especially from the American woman who loudly remarks about having had it for breakfast.

I shine my torch down the length of the room towards an opening at the other end which is nearly pitch-black. Next stop, the plague room. As I pass my way through the group, I can hear the American woman discussing with some poor soul how she had thought that the smell of the room meant we were underwater. I sigh. This is not the first time I have heard someone say that. Or the 2nd. Or the 8th.

Stepping up into the plague room, I can hear the group is

diligently following across the cobblestones behind me. I move quickly through this room so that I can cross over, grab Ivan our plastic rat off the top of the bed to my left, and head for the window. Greg, the guide from the tour ahead of me has closed the wooden shutters, but I like them open. It also allows me to conceal from the people closely behind me that I have grabbed Ivan and hidden him until his glorious moment. From the Close below, I can hear that Greg's group is making its way through Windows and out onto the Close for their requisite photographs. He must have sped quickly through the 17th century house to make up for lost time. As I turn slightly, I jump in surprise as there is a dark shadow directly behind me. I hadn't realized someone had been following behind me so closely.

Working in an underground attraction that is considered one of the most haunted locations in Scotland, your imagination can run away with you. Or at least mine does. Almost daily, tour guides are asked about their experiences with the paranormal, have we seen anything, and especially, if we think Annie, the ghost child, is still around. Being somewhat skeptical, I still keep my eyes and ears open to anything that could possibly indicating ghostly activity around me. Most of the time, all noises, sounds, and shadows can be explained. During the days, there are up to 80 people and guides on tours, with staff coming downstairs behind the scenes to change lightbulbs, complete health and safety checks, and to remove people from tours that have become unwell or uncomfortable. As there are always people moving around in the Close, it is unlikely that any strange activity can be attributed to paranormal phenomenon. But there have been times, early in the mornings for example, or when I'm in the Close alone that things have happened that can't quite be explained. I sometimes mention to tourists, if something actually scares a tour guide or makes them uneasy, then maybe, *just maybe*, something is going on.

My first thought was of a ghost. My imagination working overtime again. An apparition behind me, one only I could see, as it seemed to the others making their way through the cowshed that nothing was amiss. But this ghost spoke.

"Contact your manager. The Close is to be evacuated completely. No one here, just you and me."

This ghost is only a few inches taller than me, but built like a brick house. He is dressed entirely in black, his biceps bulge from a short sleeve shirt. The man has spoken slowly but deliberately, as if to make it clear, that whatever he was going to say wasn't going to be said twice. While I am alarmed, true fear does not course through me until the gun is pushed firmly into my stomach, becoming slightly tangled in the knotted ties of my corset. When I realize what is actually happening, my legs nearly go out from beneath me and I unconsciously reach for the windowsill behind me. Aren't guns illegal in Scotland? I feel a well of panic rising in my throat as I realize with horror that the other tourists are still making their way into the room.

The gun is pushed harder into my stomach and I gasp with the pain and I look up into the face of the madman in front of me, showing him the fear shining in my eyes.

"Use your radio. Do it. Now." This is not a request. I reach slowly behind me with my right hand and unattach the radio which is clipped to the waistband of my skirt. All tour guides carry radios, but they are used for letting management know that a light has blown out or that someone off the tour has become slightly unwell and would like to leave. Although we are thoroughly trained in emergency situations, there has been no training for something like this.

"Jonet Nimmo to Duty Manager." My voice cracks and I can't keep the well of emotion from my voice. "I have a Code Black. Repeat Code Black." The man has moved slightly to my right, in between one of the tables and the bed, and at this point is virtually out of sight from the rest of the group. Although they cannot see him, the gun pointed at my chest glints in the light of the flickering lanterns. I take a deep breath and wait as the last few climb the small step and position themselves in the room.

*   *   *

Upstairs in the manager's office, Duty Manager Derek Strom-weller tore the butcher paper stained with curry sauce from the square Styrofoam container. Dinner courtesy of the Clam Shell. One of the tour guides had gone and gotten it for him during their break. A large greasy brown sausage lie on top of a pile of salted chips, the smell of curry and vinegar permeating the small office. He leaned forward to inhale the steam rising off the chips, the tip of his tie dipping into the vibrant yellow sauce. Derek reached for a dirty fork lying next to the office sink and spears the sausage. It was halfway to his mouth when the radio crackled to life.

"*Jonet Nimmo to Duty Manager. I have a Code Black. Repeat Code Black.*"

Code Black? That radio call was reserved for only the most extremely dangerous situations in the Close. Primarily someone on the Close that was becoming violent or dangerous to other guests. They had joked when they created this code. There were other codes with various colors, red, white, blue, indicating fire, lost property, and illness in the close and these codes were used almost on a regular, day-to-day basis. The Code Black had been instituted as a precautionary code, but with the presumption that it would never actually be put into use. Derek swore as the sausage fell off the fork, bounced off his stomach and left a greasy yellow trail down his trouser leg. The sausage rolled underneath his desk and nestled against an empty bottle of Irn Bru. He grabbed for the radio, but accidentally knocked it to the ground, and by the time he managed to grab it up off the floor he was sweating, millions of situations flying through his head.

The plan was that if that someone had actually pulled a weapon or became dangerous on the Close, the tourists and guides would be evacuated, the police would be called, and but it was a tricky situation. Guides needed to let other guides and management know that there was a potentially dangerous situation in progress, but the tourists would also be able to hear what was coming in on the radios and the last thing they needed was a stampede or screaming tourists running on blind fear around the site. Had someone really, truly pulled a weapon? Carole was one of their most reliable, experienced guides and it was extremely unlikely that she would use a Code Black unless it was a valid reason. What kind of weapon? Knife? Letter opener?

Derek stumbled towards the open door and ran out into the gift shop.

7

"Ladies and gentlemen, it would appear that we have a slight situation in the Close that has come to my attention." I try to smile and brighten my voice, showing them that I confidently have everything under control and there is absolutely no reason to be alarmed. If any one of them only knew how fast my heart was racing or the nausea that gripped my stomach. The last thing I need is sheer mayhem, people running around like headless chickens in the face of danger. I am also afraid as to how the other guides will handle this. We have never practiced this before. Mirroring my fear, a voice breaks through on the radio.

"This is Stephen Boyd." Warrick Peterson. Twenty six year old theatre major at Queen Margaret University. We are all instructed to use our character names, to stay in character at all times, even when communicating over the radio. "We are outside Mary King's house. We will head straight back out to the gift shop." Bless him. He has given no indication that anything has gone wrong.

"Received." Derek sounds breathless and I know that he is probably trying to keep a calm demeanor upstairs. But he needs to phone the police, alert the City Chambers, get everyone out of the gift shop, clear the site, and then attend to the situation at hand. Absolute nightmare.

Another male voice hits the radio.

"This is Robert Ferguson, outside Mr. Chesney's house. We will be exiting out the door at the bottom of the Close. Jonet, do you need assistance?"

My stomach drops. Although Greg is a sweet guy, he's very young and new to the job at the Close. My tourists are looking at me intently, hanging on for my response. The man in the corner is standing completely still and if anyone actually had noticed him, they would mistake him for one of the mannequins in the room. But there is no mistaking the aura of threatening menace coming from that corner.

I am afraid to speak over the radio. I don't want the situation broadcast any more than it needs to be. Warrick's group is heading upstairs. One group safely out. Erica should have finished her tour already. Two groups out. Derek will handle staff members and visitors upstairs. I just need to convince Greg to get his group out of the Close and not play the hero. I decide not to use the radio. I go to the open window and lean out. I am hit in the face by a beam of yellow light coming up from the Close. Greg is shining his torch in my face.

"Mr. Ferguson, I assure you that the situation is most under control. I need you to take your group out the fire exit at the bottom of the Close and my group will be with you shortly." The light is removed from my face and in between momentarily seeing spots, I see Greg peering up at me. I give him my most confident smile and mouth 'Go'. He scurries down to his group which I can hear is becoming restless. I am relieved he has taken my advice and not questioned the situation any further.

Now it's just my group. The man at the back with the shaved head and army boots steps forward and says in broken English, "Is there a problem?" Eyes dart towards him and people seem to be holding their breath for my answer. Even the American lady is silent, holding onto her husband's arm. The German couple is wandering near the cowshed entrance, staring up at the ceiling, listening to their audio guides, oblivious. The man to my right is getting restless and I can hear him moving closer to me.

"It's just a slight health and safety problem and we will need maintenance to come in and check on it before any more tours can proceed. You will all get a full refund and a chance to come back to the Close at another time. My sincerest apologies." I am playing Jonet, talking again in my staged voice and hoping that what I have said is actually true.

My radio crackles.

"Jonet, what is your current location?" Derek is once again on the radio.

"We are in the plague room." I say back.

Enough. A voice hisses from the darkened corner. I hear him but I do not turn my head in that direction. I make a pretense of picking Ivan back up from where I have left him on the windowsill and give him a tiny squeak.

"Seems our wee friend has chewed through some wires." I wink and hope they are convinced. Several people laugh nervously and I smile back at them and wave Ivan around a bit in the air and I can see people starting to relax.

"We are going to have to evacuate the building. What I would like everyone to do is turn and go out the door beneath the large sign that says Mind Your Heads." A few people laugh at this massive sign we have hung above the low door frame and I am lightheaded with relief that they seem to have no idea of what is actually going on.

"Go through the door and take a left then follow through to your right. That is a fire exit. Once through the doors, you will be in the City Chambers and someone will be there to escort you out of the building. I will be right behind you." Once again, I have no idea if this is actually true, but I am hoping by then that Derek will have engineered something in terms of security or assistance.

People start to file out and I smile and direct them through the door. I can hear a clanking noise as the fire exit door to the City Chambers is opened. I start to walk behind them but his voice stops me.

"No. You will stay here." He steps out of the shadows, still pointing the gun at my midsection.

"Carole?" *Oh hell*. Derek is down in the Close. And using my real name. Not a good sign. I can tell the man in the corner is less than pleased with this as well as he sucks in his breath in a venomous sound.

I go to the window.

"Right here. My group are heading out the fire exit into the City Chambers."

Below me in the Close, Derek frowns up at me, hands on his hips. He is sweating profusely, beads running down his stubbled cheek. His handlebar mustache is crooked and and I smell curry and something tangier in the air. Vinegar maybe.

"Why aren't you going out with your group?" He asks and I stare at him.

"I... can't... leave." The man is moving in the room, I can hear the sound of fabric brushing behind me.

"You can't just leave your group" He stutters. "They don't

know where they are going. And I don't have anyone in the City Chambers that can meet them. And I…"

The look on my face cuts him off midsentence.

"Derek," I say very slowly. Because my back is to the man somewhere in the room behind me, I keep my hand close to my body and point my index finger at him like a gun, my thumb extended. I jerk my hand upward to mimic a gun going off and Derek's face blanches. I almost laugh aloud, because it feels like poetic justice that he should lecture me about leaving my group while I am standing at gunpoint. His head whips down to the left, towards where Greg's group has gone safely out the fire exit, then back up the Close to his right.

"Call the police." I whisper to him. Derek nods and then races back up the Close.

I am momentarily relieved that he has taken my suggestion when my arm is fiercely grabbed and I am painfully wrenched around. "That was a stupid move." he says. I can't see where he has put the gun at this point, but it doesn't matter. I know it is there.

"Doesn't matter. They will be called anyways." I stammer back to him, but he appears to not have heard me.

"Did you receive the pages?"

"Pages?"

"Don't play stupid. The pages that I left you."

"You left them?" My question is met with silence.

"Yes." I say. "I got them." I want to move closer to either the doorway into the cowshed or the door that leads to the fire exit but he is now in the middle of the room, dominating the space and I am too afraid to attempt to rush by him.

"Can you read them?"

"Yes." At this, there is a whoosh of air, as if the man has been holding his breath. He starts to come closer and I find that I am now backed up to the windowsill. There is nowhere else to go. Closer and closer he comes until he is standing less than a foot from me. I can smell the sweat on his body and the faint smell of something musky like men's cologne or deodorant. *My assailant wears perfume?* This thought goes through my head and the room is suddenly filled with a strange sound like a duck being strangled. Then with sheer terror, I cover my mouth with my hand as I realize I had actually laughed out loud. I stare wide-eyed at the man and he edges closer still, his eyes narrowed in annoyance and I close my eyes fearing the worst.

"Give me your radio." *My radio?* I fumble for it and in my nervous haste, drop it to the ground. It clatters noisily and skids out of reach, resting with a soft *bang* against one of the beds. He grunts in irritation and reaches down for it, clips it to his belt.

He grabs my wrist with his left hand, gun in his right and pulls me towards the door leading to the ghost story. I duck my head under the *Mind Your Head* sign and we are quickly through to the wine cellar. We continue moving, almost as if in a rush, and plow through the door at the opposite end of the room out onto Pearson's Close. Here, he still doesn't hesitate, and we are practically flying down the spiral staircase, my free hand grabbing desperately at my skirts so I don't trip on them. I don't know where we are going, but it dawns on me that he knows the layout of the site. Most people would get turned around down in the Close, but he moves with purpose and the confidence of someone that knows where he is going. We are in the windows room when finally he lets go of my wrist and throws me out in front of him.

Here time seems to stand still, me rubbing my sore wrist and him unclipping his backpack and setting it down on the ground. There is nothing coming from the radio and I can only imagine the chaos in the gift shop above. Have the police been called? Has the site been completely evacuated? What was that stain on Derek's suit? Vinegar? What does this guy want? And what does he mean by sending me pages with Jonet's writing? My mind whirls with questions. He is under the archway where Stewart's Close is visible beneath a plate of glass. He suddenly pounds the top of the glass with his fist. It does not break. He senses me watching him and turns.

"Sit down." He barks and waves the gun at me. I don't need to be told twice. I sit down quickly in a puddle of green satin, twisting my fingers together as I watch him put the gun in a holster at his waist. He unclasps the radio from his belt. Throws it at me. It nearly hits me in the chest.

"Tell your boss to keep everyone out of the site. That includes him."

I pause and learn this was a bad decision.

"*Do it!*" He barks.

I close my eyes and push the receiver.

"Derek, this is Carole."

"Received. What the hell is going on down there? Is there just one guy? And does he really have a gun?" Derek's voice is now high-pitched, panicky.

"Derek, I need you to…" He cuts me off.

"Are you still in the plague room? The police are on their way." *Static.* "No wait, they are here now. Carole, are you still in the plague room?" I hold my breath, willing him to shut up. The radio finally goes silent. The man under the archway is watching me with reptilian eyes.

"Derek, I need you to keep everyone out of the Close. That includes you and the police."

"I need to know your location. Is it still the plague room? I repeat, are you in the plague room? We are going to have all the fire exits cordoned off and manned with police."

This is not the answer I was wanting. I am starting to panic and Derek is starting to annoy the hell out of me.

"Derek, we are no longer in the plague room. But it doesn't matter. *Don't come down here.* No one else can come down here. And yes, there is a weapon involved." I squeak this last comment in and judging from the frown on the man's face he is less than pleased.

"What type of weapon? Where are you located now? How close to a fire exit are you?"

I open my mouth to speak, but the radio is ripped from my hand. I curl back from the hulking man standing over me. He hisses into the radio.

"If anyone else comes down into the Close, I will shoot her. Do you understand?"

"Who is this and what is your intention?" Good God. Derek is talking like he is a hostage interrogator.

The man swears and snarls into the radio. "Just shut the hell up and listen. No one, I repeat, no one is to come down in the Close. Otherwise, I will shoot her. Got it?"

"Received. However, I would like to know wh.." The man turns the radio off in disgust.

"Goddamn idiot." He hisses and clips the radio back onto his belt. He unzips his pack. I am strangely curious to know what his plans are. Have me sit and read Jonet's writing to him then kill me? How did he get it in the first place? And if the exits are blocked off, how does he think he will get out of here?

"That's Stewart's Close." He is pointing to the passage below the glass. It is as much a question as a statement. I nod.

"Where does it go?"

"I don't know."

"You don't know?" He sneers at me.

I feel my stomach turn. "No, we don't have access to it. No one goes down there."

He has already turned away from me and is walking back and forth in front of the glass plate. The lights underneath the glass plate glow up at him, casting shadows across his angled face. He gives it a sharp kick. The glass shudders but still does not break. He goes back to his backpack but suddenly we are both in darkness.

"The fuck is this? What the fuck is your boss playing at?" He shouts at me.

"I don't know." My voice wobbles and a tear slides down my cheek. I have no idea what Derek has done and I pray it's not going to get me shot. There is a loud click as the radio is torn away from the man's belt. He shouts into it.

"I don't know what fucking game you are playing but someone better turn the goddamn lights back on down here."

Derek's voice comes back over the line. "It seems that a fuse has blown in the main corridor. We are trying to get it fixed immediately. I am going to pass you over to Chief Constable Iain McKenzie who would like to ." Click. Radio goes back off.

The man is muttering under his breath and I have the brief thought that I could run back through the dark and out the fire exit. I know the Close well enough. It is a straight shot back through the room, a direct left, and I can slide on my backside down the steps, then claw my way to the stairs leading out. If only.

A light blazes in my face. The man has pulled a large torch from his bag and I blink and shield my eyes with my hand. He sets it down on the ground and it stands upright, sending a beam of light to the ceiling, which fans out and illuminates the room. A coil of rope is on the floor next to the bag and he pulls out which looks like a small sledgehammer. It goes on the ground with the rope. I see him eyeing the metal ring which is fixed to the wall next to the glass plate.

I realize then what he has planned. As if mirroring my thoughts, he picks up the hammer and positions it high over the glass plate. *Whump!* There is a slight crack but the glass holds. *Whump!* There is a louder crack and a final blow puts the hammer crashing through the plate. There is a rush of stale dusty air out of the hole and several more blows with the hammer removes the remaining glass. There is a plate on the side as well and this too is quickly demolished. Glass covers the floor like shards of ice. The air coming from Stewart's Close is cold and fear moves through me as I watch him tie the rope to the metal ring. He tugs on it a few times. It is secure. He moves towards me and my stomach coils in fear as he hauls me up off my feet and pulls me over to the chasm above Stewart's Close. I peer down. Without the glass, it looks like the mouth of a creature, waiting to swallow me up.

"Please." I say, hating the sound of my pleading voice. "If you need information about the Jonet letters, I can tell you anything. Just don't make me go down there."

He leans close to me and whispers. "Just hold still." His breath is soft on my face. I close my eyes and try to swallow the lump forming in my throat. Something is looped around my waist and I am soon tied to him. He smells strongly now of sweat and cologne and I hate being so close to him. I start to pull away, to try and flee, but I am wrenched back with an angry yank. My eyes fly open as I am suddenly wrenched off my feet and we are both now hanging in the narrow space above the underground street. Slowly, slowly we descend. I am half delirious with fear but despite the situation, am in awe at the chance to be in this unexplored space. The walls of this shaft are stone and my fingers brush them softly as I am lowered further and further down. The opening above me is slowly becoming smaller and the torch, which is between his teeth, sends light in spirals. The dust is thick in the air and I feel it coat my throat as I breathe.

I don't know the last time someone has been down here. Most of the Close was used as an air raid shelter during the Second World War and it is likely that someone working for the City Chambers used to know how to get down to Stewart's Close but as far as anyone can remember, no one has been down here for decades.

"Put your feet down." He says gruffly and I realize with horror that I had unconsciously been clinging to him. He is standing but I am still hanging about a foot off the ground and he is practically holding me up. I am in such a hurry that my feet get tangled and as he unties me from him, I end up on my face on the ground. A puff of dust rises up from where I land.

Stewart's Close extends in front of me like a black yawn. There is an opening to my right, which appears to be an entrance to a laigh house and although the light is poor, I can see blurry shapes in the darkness. Looking down the street, there are other openings on both sides, entryways to houses and workshops. The man shines the light down the Close and the light is swallowed up by the thick dusty air. I quickly stand up and brush myself off. Behind us, the Close extends up the hill towards the Royal Mile. I reach into the pouch which hangs from my waist. My own torch is in there. I click it on and shine it into the opening on my right.

The room is small, like the laigh house guests visit on the tour, but there are objects hidden under cloths. They look like crates or boxes but there are other objects as well, stacked up against the back. There is a noise behind me, a scuffling sound and I spin around. This noise has also drawn the attention of the large man beside me. He seems to ignore the fact that I have my own torch and the beams from our lights shine into another opening. It seems to extend back and although I know there shouldn't be any other side passages off the Close, the lights are swallowed by the darkness and there seems no end to the room. We stand in silence for several moments. I am holding my breath, adrenaline racing like caffeine through my veins. There it is again. The man swings around, pointing both his gun and torch into the room.

"Are there rats in the Close?" He asks.

"No."

"Can anyone else get down here?"

"No."

"Then what the hell is that." He is whispering now. I can practically feel the unconscious spike in fear radiating from his body. We stand still again, but there is nothing but silence and the yawning inky blackness before us. After a few more minutes, there is still nothing and he reaches into his pocket and pulls out a wrinkled page. He holds it one way then turns it upside down. My curiosity gets the better of me and I am leaning forward. It is a copy of a blueprint with notes scribbled to the side. It shows the warren of closes underneath the Royal

Exchange. I have seen the majority of the paperwork about the Royal Exchange but I have never seen this.

"Where did you find that?" My voice is breathy with fear and excitement.

He snatches it back out of my view, as if offended that I have been reading over his shoulder. I stand and wait.

"Stewart's Close used to extend down to the Nor Loch." He says. I am already aware of this fact. "Most of it was demolished in 1759 when they drained the Loch out to the fields and to the sea." Again, something I already knew. It is information we talk about on the walking tours we give of the city.

"But after 1759, part of Stewart's Close was diverted across several other Closes. The idea was that it would be used as a smugglers route, but it was soon closed off only to the privileged few of the city."

"No, it wasn't. That can't be. That would have been discovered when Cockburn Street was built. All of the Closes in that area were demolished."

"You're wrong."

"I'm not wrong. Otherwise Stewart's Close would have to run underneath Cockburn Street. And it doesn't."

We are arguing like children when suddenly there is a large scraping noise from behind us. I let out a small shriek and start to move blindly down the Close into the darkness.

"There shouldn't be anything down here!" I yell as I edge further away.

The man is hurrying to catch up, his light swaying to find me in the darkness.

"Just hold still damn it!" He yells after me. Catching up, he grabs my wrist again and we both peer behind us. I am shaking and as much as I hate to admit it, I am now more afraid of what is in the Close with us than of the man who has kidnapped me. He shines his light back up the Close, dust thick like smoke in the air.

"There shouldn't be anything down here." I hear myself saying again. I look up at him. He is peering with serious intent into the Close behind us and I realize that he has unclipped the gun from the holster. He is threatened by this unexpected noise.

A massive black shadow moves across the Close behind us. It was so quick that I thought perhaps that I had imagined it. I am then racing down the Close in the opposite direction, being pulled along by the man with the gun.

I am shocked at how far we run. Turns out, I am wrong. Way wrong. I had imagined the Close would just continue straight as Mary King's does, and how all the other Closes on all the other maps do. But at one point, we veer off to the right. I think we have just run into a dead end, into an abandoned house, but it just keeps going. We run further and further, the corridor twisting and winding into the darkness. After several moments, we stop and we are both gasping from the amount of dust sucked into our lungs.

"What was it?" I ask, hoping he will say it was a rat or a mouse. He doesn't answer. He has pulled the map back out and is glancing uneasily over his shoulder from where we have just come then down the page in front of him. He turns the page slightly, reaches for his torch. He shines it on the walls. They are made of stones of various sizes, and although most of the stones in Mary King's Close tend to be uniform in size and composition, it is not unusual to have an anomaly in the stonework, rubble taken from a dilapidated church or house and used in another part of the street.

In front of us, there is a small doorway that was long ago bricked up. Again, he drops his pack and extracts the hammer. After several glancing blows, one of the bricks starts to crumble. He wedges the hammer's handle in the small opening and levers it back and forth. The brick comes out in pieces and there is now a rectangular gap in the wall. Blows rain down on the bricks surrounding the opening and they start to crumble. He kicks several of them and there is finally an opening for us to squeeze through.

"Where are we now?" I ask, but I am given silence as he puts the hammer back in the bag and motions for me to go through first. I am reluctant, but at this point, I realize there aren't any other options. I again wonder what might be going on above us and whether anyone has figured out that we have long since left the accessible areas of Close. I squeeze through the opening, the rough bricks catching the lace on my dress. The man follows behind me, knocking more bricks down in the process. Here it is just as dark, but the passage we are now in appears to widen out and I can hear what sounds like a low rumbling. He grabs my wrist again and pulls me down the corridor. A few moments later, we are met by another bricked up doorway. Again, the man attacks the brick and in one breathtaking moment, one of the bricks crumbles and a shaft of pale light streams into the darkness. The man kicks through the rest of the wall and I suddenly find myself crawling up a set of stairs onto an extremely narrow street. I look up to my right and see that the close we are now on extends upwards towards the Royal Mile. Lower down to my left, a car drives slowly past on Market Street. In an instant, I know where we have come out and I forget the circumstances I have found myself in.

"I can't believe it! I know where we are! Stewart's Close

really does have another passage off of it which leads here, to Craig's Close. I can't believe no one else knows about this..."

I am cut off when there is a sharp prick at my arm and then nothing but darkness.

8

aaaaasp.

There is a something nearby. *Rassp. Rassssp.* It sounds like the dry, rasping sound a snake's scales make when it slides over a rock. I hold very still, waiting for the sound. Silence greets me. My head feels heavy and it is very dark, but I am patient. Maybe if I move just slightly, it too will move again. *Rassp.* There! It's so incredibly close. I am waiting for the sound again, when I realize there is something on my head. A towel? No, too light. A scarf? I reach up and gingerly touch my forehead with my fingertips, ignoring the snake. I am curious about this new sensation around my face. My fingertips are met with a soft fabric, slightly edged. Hmm. I have no idea what this is.

I feel funny. Like my head is full of cotton and I have pushed my body to exhaustion. My limbs feel like they are made of lead and I reach up now to touch my lips. They are dry and cracked. I frown. I can't remember what I did last night. I'm not a big drinker, haven't been drunk in years. But as I lie here, I can't think of anything else which would make me wake to such a disoriented feeling.

Rassssssssp! There it is again! I open my eyes and immediately wince. Nothing but a brilliant shiny green. A green snake? Brown, I had guessed, maybe grey but definitely not green. Why is there so much green? It flows in waves down towards my toes. It is a beautiful shade of green, illuminated by the pale sunlight peeking through the crack in the window. I stretch out my arm towards it. It is slick, cool to touch. There is something alongside it. A rich burgundy edged with yellow. Other colors swim into view. Dark brown. Cream. Pale lilac. They are slightly blurry but beautiful together. Slowly things start gathering shape and I suddenly panic. I jolt myself upright and stare in shock at the shimmering green. It is my skirt. My Jonet skirt. My hand flies to my head where I can feel my bonnet sitting skewed on my head.

Oh God. The memories of the previous day pour into my head and I am dizzy with the rush of adrenaline and fear. I look around and realize I have been lying on a large bed. An extremely large bed covered with a crimson colored satin duvet. The walls around me are covered in a pale cream paper and there are thick velvet curtains at the window tied back with ivory cord. I jump up from the bed but immediately put one hand out to steady myself. I am not wearing my shoes.

The room is small with an old wooden table near the corner of the room with a white pitcher and bowl. A small towel lies folded alongside. A tall chest is nestled on the other side of the bed, which dominates the majority of the room. There is a door to my right, the window to my left, and another door in front of me. I edge back down on the bed trying hard to catch my bearings. The blood is pounding so fiercely in my ears that I am briefly nauseated and I lean over, putting my head between my knees to fight the onslaught of sickness. I stay like this for a few moments, tears coming to my eyes and my stomach turns. Fear grips my chest like a vise. I slowly sit back up, wiping the tears away with the back of my hand. I walk slowly to the window and push back the heavy curtains. I turn away from the bright sunlight which sears my eyes. Turning back, I see I am high up off the ground. Vast fields of green stretch out from the building. There are chestnut trees, heavy with leaves obscuring a glimmer of water in the background.

Crack! I spin around, my eyes darting from side to side. Was that the floorboard? It sounded slightly faint. Again I hear it. I look frantically around the room for some sort of weapon. Next to the window is a small fireplace with an ornate grate. In a brass holder, there are several fireplace brushes and a large iron poker. I snatch the poker up and hold it close to my chest. The cracking sound I realize now is the echo of footsteps and they are gradually getting louder. Then they stop and I stare in complete horror at the door. Someone is putting a key into the lock and is turning it. Wait, had I been locked in? I raise the poker over my head, like a cricket or baseball bat. The key stops turning and the door slowly slides inwards.

Standing in the doorway is the man from the Close. He looks the same as the day before. Shortly cropped hair. Heavily muscled chest and arms. Instead of all black, he is dressed in brown cargo pants and a t-shirt. A Celtic knot tattoo curls its way around his left wrist. He stares at me for a second, eyes moving down my body, then back up to my face. He raises one eyebrow as he takes in the fact that I have brandished the iron poker and am holding it menacingly aloft over my head to show I mean business. Then he snorts and I can see a faint glimmer of surprised amusement in his eyes.

"Are you hungry?"

I can't think of anything less surprising he could have asked me. Hungry? I blink cluelessly and I forget that I am holding the poker. I frown and shake my head. He narrows his eyes at me, seemingly displeased with my answer, and despite the curling fear which sits hot in the base of my gut, my stomach rumbles traitorously. My eyes widen and I look up at the man, who is now leaning against the door jam, arms crossed over his chest, a smirk playing at the corners of his lips. I raise the poker again up over my head. He snorts again, louder this time, and it sounds momentarily as if he is choking. I realize he is trying to keep from laughing at me. He straightens and points to the closed door which is now to my left.

"Shower's in there. You'll find everything you need. Clothes are in the wardrobe." He points to the large dresser next to the bed. "Breakfast is in a half hour." He is then gone and I am standing there, trembling with shock, the poker still high up over my head.

I wait a few seconds, listening to his receding footsteps, then race to the door and slam it shut. He has taken the key and I panic, realizing I cannot lock the door. I look around wildly and run to the other side of the room where I now see that a small chair is next to the table. I shove it beneath the door knob and shake it slightly to make sure it's wedged in there tight. Then I sit back down on the bed. I am trembling, completely at a loss. Clothes? Shower? *Breakfast?* Yesterday the man had held a gun up to my face and now he is offering me the full amenities of a B&B? I am not sure what to do, what I should do, but for the moment I am afraid to disobey. My body goes into autopilot and I go to the closed door which leads to the shower.

I open the door slowly, and peer inside. The décor in the bedroom is quite ornate, most everything seemingly to be antique, but this is all-new. A large claw-footed bathtub. Two sinks set into a counter beneath a round mirror under a flood of lights. A power shower set to my right. There is a large cabinet next to the shower and opening it, I find towels, a new toothbrush in its package, and an array of soaps, shampoos, lotions, and oils.

My Jonet costume drops to the floor in a puddle of green satin and the shower spray hits me in the chest, hot and strong. My body feels too weak to stand so I sit on the floor with my knees up against my chest, letting the spray hit my back. I am afraid. I feel like a lost child and I want to go home. No one knows where I am and I can only imagine the chaos and panic the previous day's events at the Close have created.

There is an oversized bathrobe on the back of the door with a large M embroidered in gold thread on the chest. The Harvey Nichols tags are still attached to the sleeve of the robe. I reach for it, but shrink back and deciding instead on just wrapping the voluminous towel twice around me. Peeking my head out the bathroom door to make sure that the chair is still in place, I pad out over to the wardrobe and open the doors. Similarly with the bathroom, the shelves are full with stacks of folded clothing, freshly ironed, the department store tags still attached. Jenner's, Debenhams, Marks and Spencer, John Lewis. There are t-shirts. Long-sleeved button up shirts. Woolen socks. Linen trousers. I reach out and touch the material tentatively then select several garments. The trousers are too short. The t-shirt a bit tight. The sleeves of the button up too long and flap uselessly over my wrists. The socks are thick but soft and these strange clothes give me a slight feeling of comfort in my otherwise bruised world. I pin my wet hair on top of my head and tiptoe over to the door to remove the chair.

The hallway is cavernous, extending to my right and left. There is a door across from me. It is slightly open, a sliver of sunlight peeking out into the darkened hall. I am tempted to peek in. Is the man in there? I stand in front of the door for several seconds, listening. Nothing. I push the door gently with one fingertip, just so that it is wide enough for me to edge to one side and peer in. Several pieces of furniture sit in the sparse room, covered with large white sheets, but the curtains have been drawn back to let sunlight in, the air heavy with dust.

I am not sure which direction to go. There is a dead silence to the place, the only sound being my footsteps on the long carpet runner that dominates the width of the floor. I have the strange feeling of being watched, that there is someone behind me in the corridor, lurking in the shadows. I spin around, heart racing. Of course. Empty.

The hallway finally ends at a narrow staircase, dark steps descending from the darkness into a dimly lit atrium. The handrail is smooth from years of polish and peoples' hands, and I wince at the large creak which echoes as I step on the first stair. I try stepping on the edges of the runner, which is bolted down the steps with gold clasps, in order to prevent any noise, but the old wood crunches and cracks despite where I place my feet. There are many steps, spiraling down before stopping on a large flat landing which looks over a foyer at the entrance of the house. Sunlight pools white on the floors, a small marble fountain sits on a table next to the door, cracked and dry from disuse. I continue down the final few steps to the bottom, clinging on to the post at the bottom of the staircase, one final bit of encouragement and support before continuing on through the house.

I don't know where I'm going and the more I continue, the

more it feels like trespassing. I have been left to wander my way through this house, which appears to be vast in its size and grandeur, in search of my gun-wielding kidnapper who offered me the full amenities of a guesthouse. The smell of freshly ground coffee hits me, rich and intoxicating to my empty stomach. There are other smells, something hot and greasy, something fresh and perhaps slightly burnt. There is a clatter of crockery and the soft sound of something sizzling coming from my right. I bravely cross over and push through the swinging door from behind the sound has come.

The kitchen is as large a room as I have yet seen in this house. Dark waxed wood dominates the space in the form of floor to ceiling cupboards, and a stainless steel refrigerator lurks in the shadowy corner off to the right. There is an island in the middle of the room with wooden bar stools pulled up to the counter.

My captor is standing over a large stove frying bacon. He doesn't appear to have heard me come in and I stand there nervously, waiting for the moment when he realizes he is no longer alone. He reaches for a small carton of eggs and deftly cracks one into the pan. A large glass cafetiere of coffee sits steaming next to a container of fresh orange juice. Moments which seem like ages pass and I shift my weight slightly to give him a subtle hint that I am in the room with him. I don't want to make any sudden moves, fearing his unexpected response. I jump suddenly as toast pops out of the toaster with a metallic clang and feel my face redden and my skin crawl as he slowly turns and notices me. We stand, not saying a word, when he motions to the bar then turns back to the sizzling pan.

The bar is too close to him for my liking. I am afraid to go forward but afraid to anger him, so I move slowly and stand next to the bar rather than sit down at it. Up close, I notice that there are several jars of jam on the table with a plate of fresh butter, a bowl containing cut melon, and a small sugar bowl. I am shocked at the delicacy at which the silverware has been arranged in front of me and even more shocked to see a spray of heather arranged in a crystal vase on a side table. He turns around and sets a plate down. Toast, bacon, and a square Lorne sausage swimming in egg yolk. He sweeps his arm in a 'help-yourself' gesture and then turns and leaves the room through a door to my left.

I am standing there, confused, lost, helpless, starving, the thought of combining a large breakfast with the adrenaline racing through my body making me nauseous. I sit down at the table and for the next 20 minutes, work my way through the toast, pick at the meat and eggs, devour the majority of the melon and half the container of orange juice. I am grateful and ashamed that I have eaten so much, and am filling a mug with coffee and milk when he comes back into the room. My face flames as he notices my near-empty plate and comes over to take it from me to take it to the sink.

"Thanks." I whisper to his turned back as he runs water over the greasy plate. He grunts in response, places the plate in the drainer, and wipes his hands on a towel. He turns and rests his hip against the counter, arms folded over his chest. He is watching me intently, power radiating from his body. My eyes drop to my lap, my face on fire.

"The page I left at the Close. You said you could read it."

"The page?" I ask, my head whipping up to meet his gaze.

"The photocopy."

"Yes, I did and I can but…"

"What does it say?"

"I haven't really had a chance to look at it all the way through. I mean, I recognized the handwriting but…"

"You've had it for several days and you haven't even looked at it? Didn't you realize what it is?" His voice is impatient, exasperated.

"I only got it yesterday. And my manager brought it to me right before I went on tour so I didn't have much time." I am rambling, nervous.

"I left it three days ago." His voice is angry, growling.

My face flames again. I shake my head.

"Management must have forgotten about it." My voice wavers in my pathetic attempt of an apology.

He lets out a loud sigh then turns back to the sink. It appears he is counting under his breath. I bite my lower lip and wait for him to respond. Will he shout? Break something?

"You are studying at the University." His change in discussion throws me off guard.

"Y-y-yes."

"A PhD in history. The letters from the Museum. From the woman you play at the Close. Janet."

"Jonet." I whisper. He knows too much. Knows about the Jonet letters. Knows about my research on them. And based on the sheet he left at the Close, maybe more about Jonet Nimmo than I do.

"Whatever." His voice is rough, sharp, commanding. "This is the way this is going to work. I have something I need you to you to read. And you need to read it quickly. Then after I have the answers I need, I'll take you back to Edinburgh."

That was it? He held me at gunpoint, broke through Stewart's Close, and kidnapped me from Edinburgh so I could *read* something for him?

I nod like a bobble head puppet. "What is it? Another letter?"

"Come with me."

I slide quickly off the stool, nearly knocking it to the floor in my haste, and scurry after him. I follow him into a small corridor and quickly turn off to the left into a well-lit study, sunlight streaming through the two streaky sash windows directly opposite the door. A massive mahogany table is hidden by piles of paper which upon further inspection I find are maps, blueprints, illustrations, and sheets with heavy scrawls. A cup of pencils sits half hidden in the middle of the desk along with several books, a magnifying glass, and an empty tea cup. On a small table next to the windows is a bottle of Glenmorangie, the amber liquid casting a swath of light the color of rich caramel across the floor.

The man rifles through several sheets of paper, then pauses after extracting the page he has searched for. He shoves the piece of paper towards me. "Read this."

The paper he has thrust into my hands is a photocopy, slightly earmarked at the edges, with uneven lines of old-fashioned handwriting across the front. A chill runs through me. The script is unmistakably Jonet's. Soft, loopy, angular. I have stared at it for hours, in coffee shops, my flat, and at the museum and I am certain I haven't seen this letter. Or maybe this is a copy of one of the four that I haven't transcribed yet?"

"Where did you get this?"

The man frowns at me. "Doesn't matter. Read it."

"I can't."

"What the hell do you mean you can't? You just damn well told me you could."

"Yes, I can but,"

"Then why can't you read it?" His tone is darkening, turning angry.

I take a deep breath. "I can read it, but it will take a bit of time. It's in Old Scots. I will have to transcribe it."

"And you can do that?"

I nod again and he relaxes slightly at this. Turning towards a locked cabinet on the far wall, he takes a small key from his pocket and opens the door, reaching in to extract a small book, wrapped in cloth. He slightly hesitates, transferring the book nervously from hand to hand before setting it gently on the table. He searches through a stack of paper on another table nearby and pulling aside several pages, holds one up.

"Do you know what this is?"

It is another photocopy. Faintly, I can see that it is an illustration of a heart topped by a jeweled crown. I narrow my eyes, then shake my head. He holds up another. This time in the sketch, the chain has been added, but it still doesn't give me any idea as to what it is. Another page brings the necklace to life in color, the heart a rich plum color, the crown gold with three colored stones, one red, one green, and one blue. He shows me several variations of the same picture but each time, I shake my head. I have no idea what this necklace is or how it could relate to Jonet's writing.

This seems to frustrate him and he throws the pages down onto the pile and runs his hand through his short-cropped hair. He turns away from me momentarily, placing his hands on his hips and staring out the window. My stomach churns nervously and I am afraid once again.

"Get yourself another cup of coffee, then come back." He says and it is given as a command. I do not want more coffee but I do not argue. I go back the way we came, into the kitchen, where the coffee is still hot in the cafetiere. My eyes prickle with tears and my hands shake as I pour the coffee, spilling it over the edge, splashing it to the countertop. A clumsy dash of milk and a large spoon of sugar and I am racing quickly back to the study.

The table has been cleared. The books piled on the floor next to the table legs, the pages stacked in neat piles around the room. A fire has been started in the grate and the wood crackles and pops. The faint aroma of woodsmoke fills the room and although I feel the warm air, it does nothing for the cold sensation that runs down my spine. An armchair has been pulled up to the table. I set my cup down and stand like a soldier, awaiting instructions. I can feel the caffeine from the first coffee hitting my bloodstream, my legs wobbling like jelly and adrenaline sears my veins.

"Sit down." I fall heavily into the chair, bumping the table with my leg, the coffee sliding over the rim of the cup and pooling alongside. I look at the puddle of brown liquid in horror, then looking up to see that he is still standing with his back to me at the window, wipe up the liquid with the sleeve of my borrowed shirt. The man starts to pace the room.

"I have a document which I need you to translate. Quickly. If you need anything, just ask. After you have finished, I will take you back to Edinburgh. Until then, you will remain here. There is information I am in dire need of, and from what I have been told, you are the one I must get it from."

I stare at him, uncomprehending. What information? What document? Another Nimmo letter? Something else? What could he possibly need it for? While historically informative, Jonet's letters had only discussed daily life in 17th century Edinburgh, information I couldn't see this man urgently needing. And how did this relate to the necklace he had shown me earlier?

"What document is it?" I ask. He turns and points towards the cloth-bound document on the edge of the table. Near it is a pair of white cotton gloves. Whatever this is, it is valuable enough that he knows that it must not be touched by bare hands. I slip the gloves on and reach for the bundle, unwrapping the parcel slowly, dust rising in small puffs off the aged material.

It is a small thin book, bound in dark cracked leather. One corner appears to have been scorched, the leather blackened and curling. The spine has deteriorated, due to frequent bending and the binding is creased. It gives off the musty, earthy smell of an old book and I faintly smell smoke, although whether this is emanating from the charred corner of the book or the lit fireplace, I am not sure. Opening the book to the first page, I find there is a hint of foxing along the edge, the rust-brown stain in tiny spots along the crease. This type of staining is typical of old documents, whether it be books, certificates, or manuscripts, and although foxed documents typically can be repaired or bleached, it is not without the risk of damage to the paper or ink. The page is blank except for a small J written in fading black ink in the upper right hand corner.

The majority of the pages are yellowed and brittle. Several of them threaten to separate from the binding, and I am careful to turn them gently. Each page is filled with the writings of Jonet Nimmo. This is not another set of letters. This is a diary. *Her diary*. I am shocked and momentarily excited, at the book's existence and the thrill of delving deeper into the story of her life.

"Where did you get this?" My voice is a breathy whisper.

"It doesn't matter where it came from. Within that," He

points to Jonet's diary like something which could bite him. "Are the details of where this necklace may be. And I want it. Find it."

I stare at him, my mind twisting around his words. Then he is gone.

The room is strangely silent except for the soft hiss of the fire and the quiet, faithful tick of the ancient grandfather clock in the corner. I let out a sigh and stare at the diary in front of me. The initial feelings of elation have faded and I am left with a sinking feeling in the pit of my stomach. What has suggested seems nearly impossible. To read through an entire 17th century diary, looking for details describing the location of a necklace, which may or may not exist? What if Jonet never wrote about the necklace, only drew it? And what if the drawings are not Jonet's rather from someone else?

I sit back in the chair, anxiety twisting my gut. I look around. The room is darkly paneled, a large watercolor of Alexander Naysmith's Nor' Loch and Edinburgh Castle in a gilt frame, prominent on the eastern wall. Dusty books sit on shelving behind glass cabinets on the remaining walls. An old rifle hangs over the fireplace. There is a brass label below it, but from where I sit, I cannot read it. The smell of smoke from the fire is starting to mask the smells of lemon and wax which had initially caught my attention upon first entering the room.

My eyes are drawn back to the diary. I feel a strange pulling and before I know it, I am reaching for it.

9

March 1633

Today Mother's brother came to visit us. I have never met him before but he seems quite pleasant. He is very tall and has red hair. He does not live in Edinburgh, but lives up in the North. He brought everyone gifts, my present is a diary. Mother says it will help me practice my penmanship but I do not want to use it for that. Uncle says it is for writing down stories and secrets. I prefer that idea much more...

The clock chimes a solemn one o'clock. I have been working for several hours. I push back from the table and take off the gloves. Pressing my hands into my lower back rewards me with several satisfying pops and I lean forward to stretch. The door into the room flies open and I straighten with a start, the blood rushing painfully to my face.

Colin's mouth is open as if he was going to say something, but my startled look and red face confuse him and he is momentarily speechless.

"What are you doing?"

"Just stretching. My back is a bit cramped." I mumble this

to him, my face flaming hotter. He simply continues to stare at me then turns away.

"Come. I'll get you some lunch."

I am led back through the dark narrow passage to the kitchen, the walls seeming to press in on me. At the table is a plate with a sandwich. He motions towards the table then after watching me settle in the chair, leaves the room.

So this is the way it will be. I will work, he will feed me. And when, someday, I find the answers he wants, he will let me go.

The sandwich is ham. I hate ham sandwiches but I am too afraid to be picky. Thankfully it washes down easily with large mouthfuls of Coke. It is soon followed by a pear, a carton of yogurt, and a hardboiled egg.

Although I am finished with my lunch, the man has not returned. My insides are churning with the food and with my fearful anxiety. I am confined, trapped, claustrophobic. I need fresh air.

I head back out to the main entrance, past the fountain, and to the main doors. Heaving one open, a blast of cold air hits me square on. It is crisp, sharp, and I inhale deeply, drinking it in like someone ravaged by thirst. The wind blows hair into my face and it is so cold that tears prickle my eyelids. It is only September, but the air is icy, foretelling an early approaching winter.

I am standing on a small stone landing, at the top of three stairs which broaden out as they extend down to the drive. On either side of the steps is a large stone lion, face fixed into a permanent scowl. I sit down on the top step and set the can of Coke down beside me.

At the front of the house is a circular drive which curls back out to the left and disappears into a blanket of thick, dark forest. Across from the house is a field, overgrown with weeds and thistles. There are several large oak trees as well, their leafy edges turning yellow, one broken and splintered from a recent lightning strike.

From my seat, I crane my neck around to look at my temporary prison. The door I have just come out of has two large round iron handles on the front and above the doorway, there is a family crest and lion rampart carved into the stone. On one side of the coat of arms is a thistle and on the other side a simple rose. There is a bell pull to the right of the door

I go down the steps out into the drive and turn back around. My prison is a castle. It is grandiose, stately, a manor house which towers high into the clear Scottish sky. There is a large crenellated tower on the southern side of the building, with fake arrow slits and heads carved deep in the stone. The main section of the house extends to the north with a slanting tile roofline, long rectangular windows, and a balcony which extends over the main entrance. A rotten wine barrel, overturned in its disuse, lies to the right of the stairs. In the pale autumn sunlight, there is a rosy glow to the stonework and it is silent except for the rush of the wind in the trees and the distant roar of a passing plane, its contrail streaking white into sapphire sky. Above me, crows wheel and twist in the brisk air, their sharp screech renting through the silence.

"What the hell do you think you are doing?"

I have craned my neck so far to the left to watch the crows overhead that when I hear Colin's voice, I nearly stumble in my surprise. His face is dark, angry, panicked. He looks at the can of Coke on the steps and then scowls.

"I wasn't going anywhere. I needed fresh air. I was just

looking at the house." My words tumble out, stumbling over each other in haste to explain my absence from the kitchen.

He harrumphs then stoops to pick up the can and disappears back into the house. My shoulders slump and taking one last look, I head dejectedly back inside.

10

October 1645

The plague has once again hit Edinburgh. William says we are safe here, miles from the city where the foul pestilence ravages the streets and grips people in a vise of death. There are stories, terrible stories of people, left in their homes, unable to leave, sick and dying. They have set out to enforce quarantines; afflicted families must stay in their homes until the requisite six weeks has passed or they die first. Most people do not survive the quarantine.

They say it starts with fever, your body bathed in sweat as your muscles are racked with pain and convulsions. Purging of the body soon follows and you cough so wretchedly that your insides start to burn. With some, their fingers, toes, and tongue turn black; however, once it reaches this stage, it is normally too late. Many experience large blisters swelling from various areas on the body before popping, the foul yellow fluids releasing from the wound and poisoning the blood. There is one man, Dr. George Rae, who has been in charge of aiding the sick, but people are dying so frequently, he cannot attend to them quickly enough.

The streets are dead except for the men called foul clengers. These are the city's plague cleaners, large men who have once before survived the plague. They go into the homes, remove any bodies, and leave donations of bread, wine, and firewood for those too sick to leave their beds. They have started to burn broom in the homes, in an attempt to remove the miasmas which are causing the sickness. This has apparently not been entirely successful, as fires are raging in the tightly-confined closes. People have been caught trying to leave the city gates, to flee from the sickness, only to be put in prison or the stocks for the unintentionally spreading the disease outside the walls. Children found playing in the streets are being whipped alongside the Mercat Cross and parents caught hiding a sick child have been branded.

Shipments have stopped being delivered to the city. The port has been closed and animals found in the streets are immediately destroyed. The people have been left to fend for themselves until the sickness fades.

It is a barbaric thing, to prevent people from leaving their homes and their city to save their lives, but William says that there is no other option. If it were not for the quarantines, the plague could spread further, killing us all. Despite his reassurances that we will be spared, fear grips my heart. The plague sits like a black, festering cloud over Edinburgh, a shroud which consumes everything living in its path. I have not received any news from Euphemie, William, or Alexander in over a fortnight's time. I hope this does not mean the worst.

*   *   *

It has been the longest day of my life. I lie in the massive bed, staring up at the delicately carved ceiling, its garlands and floral bouquets looping from one corner to the next. I am exhausted, yet my mind is racing. The first two entries have not yielded any information about the necklace. I am disheartened, fearful, exhausted. I hope that tomorrow will give me the information I need.

11

The next morning starts very much like the first. After breakfast, I am herded back into the study. Several hours later, I am leafing through the diary when the man appears in the doorway. "Carole." My name is spat out like a gunshot. I am immersed in the diary and have not heard him arrive so I jump, startled. "Come with me." I get up, pushing away from the table so quickly that I knock the chair over backwards in the process.

"This is against my better judgment." He growls and turns his back on me. I hurry to catch up. I can only imagine *what* is against his better judgement. Where are we going?

We pass through a part of the house I have yet to see. Blue and white Chinese vases on pedestals, marble sculptures, and art pieces flash by until we come to a set of heavy oak doors. He turns to face me.

Eyebrows heavy, face deep in shadow, the man opens his mouth as if to say something, but then hesitates. For a moment, his face falls and I see a glimmer of pain and vulnerability. But a second later, the angry mask is back in place and he sighs loudly in frustration. He pushes one of the doors open and stands quietly while I enter, then pauses to shut it silently behind us. His manner has changed. He is softer, quieter. The room opens to what appears to be a large ballroom; pale blue carpet spans the expanse of the space. Sunlight streams through several massive windows on the other side of the room and dust motes dance in the pale light. The room feels empty and I can see that there is one chair near the windows, a white blanket thrown across its back. Daisies in a tall crystal vase sit on the ledge and out the windows and I can see an expanse of green and the glint of sun off a body of water.

I am confused. Although the room holds a sweetened, medicinal tang, the room is empty. Why would bringing me here be a bad idea? Then the man spoke.

"Carole's here, my love". His voice is soft, gentle, unlike the rough cadence I was used to hearing. A moment passes and there is a sound like a soft sigh. Across the room, there is a low rustling sound and a flicker of movement. If it hadn't been for a slight change in the light, I might not have seen it at all. I find myself moving forward, although whether this is from prompting from the man behind me or my own volition, I do not know. The walk across the ballroom takes an eternity. Moments later I am standing in front of the windows. A knot forms in my stomach and my skin grows cold.

There is a woman sitting in the chair. Dressed in white linen, a white shawl around her shoulders, she looks up at me and shock ripples through my gut. Although she is young, it is no secret she is ill. Her body is shrunken and wasted. There are dark circles under her eyes, her skin pale and thin, her hands veiny and withered. She has no hair or eyebrows but none of this takes away from one thing. She is still breathtakingly beautiful. Her face is heart-shaped and her eyes, unlike the rest of her body, are vibrant, sea green and gold in color, and sparkling with excitement. She leans forward to me and reaches out a hand. I awkwardly shuffle forward and take her hand in mine. It is cool, dry, soft.

"Carole. I am so excited that you are here. Colin, won't you fetch Carole a chair?"

A chair appears and I find myself sitting in it across from this ethereal woman. Colin has gone to stand beside her and he leans forward to give her a kiss on the cheek. She reaches up and gently caresses his stubbled cheek and for a moment, time stops and nothing but their love swirls around us.

I am uncomfortable, embarrassed, and I look away, my eyes resting on a silver frame on the window ledge. It is of a man and woman on their wedding day, their faces alight with joy, the woman's lacy gown spread out on the grass behind her. *Colin and Laura Kinross, June 15, 2009.* Colin raises her skeletal hand, kisses her open palm and then leaves. Golden-green eyes turn on me.

"I am so sorry I wasn't able to meet you when you arrived yesterday. I'm afraid I wasn't quite feeling up to it."

I open my mouth to speak but only a croaking sound comes out. I nod instead.

"I've been looking forward to you coming to visit us for such a long time. It is wonderful to finally meet you." She reaches forward to clasp my hand again. A soft wave of perfume stirs the air.

"You are much prettier in person than in your picture."

"My picture?"

"Yes, the one in the paper from the Museum gala."

Laura reaches to the side table and lifts a small notebook. From the creased pages, she pulls out a clipped newspaper article and hands it to me. It is all too familiar. The picture centers on Vivienne Stuart-Whyte, her holding up one of the letters encased in its protective sheath, with the Museum director standing nearby, applauding. I am in the corner of the photo, like the proverbial wallflower, holding a glass of champagne and trying to inconspicuously blend in. The same newspaper article is tacked on my bedroom wall. I hand it back to her.

"Thank you."

"I'm so pleased you have agreed to help us. So kind of you to take time from your studies, I know how busy you must be. While you are here, you must let Colin know if you need anything to make your stay more comfortable. My home is your home."

I do not know what to say to this. So many thoughts are racing through my mind. It is obvious that the truth of the situation has been withheld from her, but I am not the one who is going to break this fragile web of happiness. I do the only thing I can think of. I nod like a bobble head doll and smile.

"I appreciate that." I have no idea where those words have come from, but I know they are the right thing to say. Laura's smile could block out the sun.

"Has Colin given you the tour of the house?"

"Not yet. I've been working on the diary."

"That naughty man! Making you work from the start and not even giving you a tour of our lovely home. I will ask him to show you around after lunch. I assume he has told you everything about my family and the diary though?"

"Um, he might have left a few things out. I'm not sure. Perhaps you could tell me?"

"Well," Laura leans forward, radiance spreading throughout

her face. "Several months ago, I came across a small chest that was up in the attic. Wait, perhaps I should back up. You see, several years back, my grandmother passed away, and as the only grandchild, she left her entire estate to me. Colin and I had been living in a small flat in Glasgow at the time, but decided we would move out here. Colin had just returned from being overseas with the army and wanted some time to enjoy married life and get away from the rush of the city.

After we moved in, there was so much to sort through. My grandparents were avid collectors of Scottish antiques, most of them dating back to the 17th and 18th centuries. Some things went to charity, some things we got rid of, but the majority of things, we kept. My grandmother was immensely interested in Scottish history and had spent a lot of time tracing our family's roots back to the late 16th century. She had apparently gone weekly into Edinburgh to meet with a gentleman at Scotland's People who helped her develop the genealogical information. Needless to say, over the years, she had accumulated a large amount of information on our family. You should have seen how many boxes of papers there were!

Colin and I were trying to make our way through all the artifacts, to put them together in one room when we found a small chest up in the attic. It was hidden away underneath one of the eaves, completely covered with cobwebs and dust. Who knows how long it had lain up there!

As with everything else, we brought it down and cleaned it but we didn't open it until several weeks later. In the chest was the diary. We could read Jonet's name on the inside cover and the odd word here or there, but for the most part, it was a mystery to us. But then we found the drawings, tucked away inside the pages of the diary. I can't tell you how excited I was.

They were so beautiful, so incredibly detailed, and I looked through the chest, hoping that perhaps it was nestled somewhere at the bottom. It wasn't of course, but I rather hoped that it was somewhere, secreted in amongst Grandmother Sinclair's other things. We never found it, and I thought that perhaps, the location of the necklace might be somewhere in the diary. That Jonet had written about it and perhaps mentioned what had happened to it.

It frustrated me, my inability to read the diary. Who knew? The necklace could be right under our noses and we would never know it. Then one day Colin told me he had an idea. There was a woman, a student in Edinburgh, who was trained to read old documents. He showed me the article from the paper and I knew at once we must implore you to help us. As I couldn't travel to Edinburgh, I asked Colin to invite you here. And here you are!"

"And here I am." My voice is hollow, disbelieving.

"So what do you think? Can Jonet's mystery necklace be found?" Laura's brilliant green eyes stare at me with an unnatural intensity.

I struggle to clear my throat.

"I, um, am not sure." My voice has taken on a high, strained pitch. Thoughts race through my head.

"Will you come back later this afternoon? I would like very much to hear about what you have discovered so far."

"I can't promise I'll know much."

Laura waves a hand in the air gaily. "No worries, my dear. There is time yet. Colin!" She looks up, joy radiating from her face.

Colin has silently entered the room and appeared at her elbow. He holds a fresh vase of daisies in one hand. He places them in the window and then brushes her cheek with his fingers.

"Carole will help us, darling. She's wonderful. She has found out so much already!" Laura is beaming up at Colin, a look of happiness radiating from her gaunt features.

"I always knew she would." Colin does not look at me when he says this.

I mumble that I should probably get back to work and leave the room. A range of emotions flood me as I head back to the study. I am confused, overwhelmed, relieved, angry. I pace back and forth in the confines of the small room, stopping to stare out the window. Colin had kidnapped me, brought me here simply for the love of his sick wife. I turn and jump slightly. Colin stands in the doorway, leaning against the jam, hands in his pockets, a sad and pained look on his face.

"Colin." I spit his name out like something foul in my mouth. There is a slight flicker of emotion in his eyes, but aside from that he does not move. We stand across from each other, a silently waged battle. I cannot stand the silence. It impregnates the room, leaving the air heavy, suffocating.

"I'm sure I don't have to tell you that Laura is dying." I didn't expect him to speak first. His voice is hollow and the weight of his words hits me like a slap.

"No, I..I know, I mean..." I am caught off-guard. I am stuttering and don't know what to say. "But you lied. You lied to her." My words sound immature, pathetic.

He shrugs and crosses his arms, looks at the floor. Moments pass and when he looks back up at me, his face is ashen.

"Do you know what it is like?" A hoarse whisper, threaded with desperation.

"What... what is like?"

"Do you know what it is like?" Colin repeats himself, as if he hasn't heard me. His eyes are vacant.

"Do you know what it is like to have your whole world crash down around you? To watch the only person you love fade before your eyes? To watch them fight the pain and suffering knowing they cannot win?"

It is like being punched in the gut. I blink rapidly. My anger has gone, released like a deflated balloon and hot tears have formed in my eyes. There is a knot in my throat and I cannot swallow. I lose the battle. One lone tear scalds my cheek.

"I'm sorry."

Colin shrugs again and with a sigh of defeat and resignation, uncurls himself from the doorway. He passes the small side table near the fireplace to stand at the window. He stares out, seeing nothing.

"Laura has always held a deep interest in her family's history. Several months after her grandmother died, she ran across paperwork which had been compiled, tracing the family line back through to the late sixteenth century in Edinburgh. For days, she poured over the records, going through everything. In the bottom of one of the boxes was a small chest. In it was all that."

He does not motion towards the diary and information spread across the surface of the table but I know what he is referring to.

"She was so excited. She couldn't read a bit of it, but that didn't stop her imagination from running wild. Inside the diary, Laura found Jonet's name."

Again, I know what he is referring to. Jonet's signature is remarkably clear, fluid, and perfectly legible on the inside cover.

"Laura went back through the records and there she was.

Daughter of Mary King. At the time, we had no idea about Mary King's Close, its history and the connection to Jonet. Laura was just so excited to have the diary of one of her ancestors and be able to accurately trace the line back. Despite our best efforts, we couldn't read anything written in the diary except for the odd word. We found the watercolors tucked into the pages of the diary. For weeks, it was all she talked about. The necklace, where it might be, if it still survived, and perhaps it was even in one of the boxes still in the attic? We searched but never found it. Laura starting pouring over the internet trying to find information on a woman named Mary King that lived in Edinburgh during the 17th century. We didn't expect to find much. Mary King is such a common name. Neither of us could believe it when the first thing that came up was the website about the Close. We realized that this Mary King was not only the same Mary King from Laura's family, but one of the tour guide characters was actually based on the woman who wrote the diary."

Colin stops talking and running a hand through his disheveled hair, turns to pour a large measure of Glenmorangie into a glass. Two fingers are quickly splashed into the crystal glass, sticky with residue from the previous night's tipple. I don't say anything, just hold completely still, holding my breath. My head is spinning. Laura is the living relation to Jonet Nimmo and Mary King.

"Then Laura got sick." Colin is staring into the empty fireplace, a vacant, haunted look in his eyes. His voice is starting to crack and I can feel a strange tension slowly and ominously building in the room.

"We had every intention of going to the Close, to visit the site, take the tour, to ask questions. We thought we would wait and go as soon as Laura got a bit better." There is a pause.

"But she didn't get better." The hand holding the glass of whisky has started to shake and the golden liquid sloshes, threatening to spill over the rim. He is squeezing the glass so tightly I am afraid it will break.

"And even though Laura got sicker, she would talk about the diary, how she wished she could read it and how she wished she knew more about the necklace. Then one day I ran across that newspaper article about the letters being donated to the museum. You know, the one talking about you and how you were going to read them as part of your studies and how you actually played the character of Jonet at the Close."

The knot in my throat threatens to choke me when I try to speak so I simply nod.

"She could hardly believe it. You were the answer to all her questions! For the first time in weeks, Laura showed signs of improvement. She said she would write you a letter, asking you for your help, if you could read a part of the diary and inform us about the necklace. She even mentioned that in return for your help, you could take the diary and use it as part of your research. She was so happy, so full of hope."

"So I told her I would arrange it. I told her that I would send a letter to you." There is an air of finality in his voice.

"Why didn't you simply ask?" My voice is a strained, sad whisper.

"Laura then suddenly took a turn. I was so afraid that you would say no. That you would say you couldn't get the time off of work, that you were too busy, or some other reason. Some other excuse. I couldn't risk that."

"She doesn't have a lot of time left. I had one chance, *one last chance* to make her happy. I wasn't going to chance the possibility that you wouldn't help us. So, I lied. I told Laura I would contact you. Told her that I would arrange for you to visit. And instead I started coming to the Close, finding out more about you, when you were working, and what the site was like. I must have gone on a half a dozen tours.

I couldn't think of any other way. I was running out of time and I wanted to do this one last thing for my wife before she was gone." The glass is empty, Colin is back at the window.

"I would have helped you." I say to Colin's back. It is a pitiful thing to say, but I can think of nothing else.

"I suppose it doesn't really matter now, does it? You are here now. And at this point, you won't say no."

"I won't?"

"No. You won't" Colin turns to me, hands back in his pockets, pain and anguish in his eyes.

"Because if you changed your mind now, you'd have to go upstairs and explain to my dying wife that you'd rather not help her anymore."

"That's not fair." I whisper.

"Go and tell that to her."

12

October 1639

The countryside is beautiful but I am far from the city and William leaves for days at a time, leaving me alone with the servants. I wanted to remain in the city so that I may visit Mother but William detests the filth of the city and so we moved here four days after the wedding. The house is lovely and well-furnished but it does not feel yet like home. The servants are wary of me, and I of them and while they do not object to my commands, they do not consider me the Lady of the House, as it has only been a year since William's mother, Lady Louisa, has passed away.

The house is large and filled with elaborate furnishings, mostly procured by William during his visits to London and Paris. In our sitting room there is a grand Arras tapestry, a Turkish rug, and tea is served midafternoon with tiny sugared cakes arranged in silver cake baskets. I am in awe of my new luxurious surroundings. It will take time to get used to such extravangance.

There is a large rose garden on the estate, designed by William's mother, and it gives a swath of color to the vast green fields surrounding the house. There is a strange statue in the garden and I have learned it is called a sundial. Many of the wealthy with private gardens in the city have these and William purchased one for our garden. It is made of slate and is used to tell time based on the angle of the sun. William tried to explain it to me the other day, but I must confess, I was rather more distracted by being in his presence than concentrating on the dial itself.

He constantly astounds me with tales from his overseas journeys. He tells me that there are many new goods coming in to Leith Harbor from Spain, France, the Mediterranean and the Low Countries. Although William is gone frequently, traveling back and forth to Edinburgh, he always brings me something home from the city which has recently arrived. Plums from Italy, fur-lined gloves from Russia, a painted fan from Paris.

The other day he brought me the strangest thing, something I have never seen before. It is a bright yellow fruit, with a hard, waxy peel. It is called a lemon and the smell is divine. They are arriving in Edinburgh in crates of 10,000 fruits per box. I am told it is best used if the juice is added to a pitcher of water, and it truly does make the water ever so lovely to taste.

If I am honest, I am excited about my new life here. William is a wonderful man and although I miss my mother dearly, it is only a two hour carriage ride back to the city. William has promised we will go to Edinburgh at the end of the month.

I sit back and stare at the entry I have just completed. Extraordinary. So much detail, so much exquisite information about life in 17th century Scotland. A part of me cannot wait to share this with Laura, but I am also afraid. Afraid to disappoint her and afraid of how to act after the scene with Colin this morning.

I stand and gather my notes. Colin is using me. We both know it. He has me between a rock and a hard place and he knows I will stay until the diary is transcribed and I have gleaned every scrap of information I can out of it. This is simply because I cannot, *will not* look a dying woman in the eye and selfishly refuse my efforts.

The study door swings outwards.

"Laura has asked me to make sure you get a full tour of the house, but I have other things to do. You can just wander around the place at your leisure." He stops talking, waiting for my response. I nod.

"I will take you back upstairs to see Laura after lunch." I then find myself alone.

Leaving Jonet's diary behind, I go back to the main atrium where the dry fountain sits like a sentinel at the entrance. While I am uncomfortable with freely wandering through someone's home, I am anxious to see what treasures are hidden away in this vast estate.

There are doorways going off in various directions, like the spiraling arms of a nebula. There is one to the left of the entrance. It is merely a small alcove, a cloakroom, with several dusty coat hooks set into the wall. Another doorway to the right empties into a sunlit room, devoid of furniture, nothing but heavy curtains and an old fireplace grate.

Moving around the corner of the staircase, I push the door

open to reveal another long corridor. I imagine it mirrors the hallway upstairs. Immediately, there is a room open to my left.

It is a large, airy room with floor to ceiling windows looking out to an expanse of garden and a low stone wall at the edge of the manicured grass. An oriental rug covers the majority of the wooden flooring and a crystal vase of pink and white alstromerias sit on a large round table in the middle of the room. The room is softly feminine, with armchairs arranged around the table, a small recessed alcove with a painter's easel next to a low divan set underneath one of the windows, the seat a sweep of pink fabric with tiny embroidered flowers.

There is a small writing desk on one side of the room with an ornate silver inkwell, several sheets of aged paper, and a postcard from London dated 1976. A black quill pen, lies to one side, the nub worn and blunted. It is beautifully arranged, and leaves the feeling that the writer has simply stepped out for a cup of tea and will be back any moment to continue their correspondence.

Over the fireplace, there is a large watercolor of a woman. She is dressed in a flowing pink gown, several strands of white pearls looped around her neck and hanging down to the middle of her stomach. Her auburn hair is coiled on top of her head, several strands falling down to tease the nape of her neck. She holds a book in one hand, a spaniel lying asleep at her feet.

The crowning glory of the room is a glossy grand piano, the lid covered in silver frames. The photographs are black and white; a woman in a vintage wedding dress, an elderly man with a cane crouched next to a black terrier, a glossy Rolls Royce. There are raspberry colored goblets set along the window ledge and the sun casts rosy shafts of light across the floor.

Across the room, a doorway opens onto an adjoining room.

It is markedly different, smaller, dark, heavy, and masculine. I imagine I can smell cigar smoke, still lingering in the air.

A mahogany and gold leaf clock silently ticks next to a brass barometer on the mantelpiece of an Aberdeenshire granite fireplace. Above the fireplace are more black and white photos; Clydesdale horses pulling a wooden cart, a shepherd walking faithfully behind a herd of sheep down a dusty road, men on horseback surrounded by dozens of dogs, their tails high eagerly awaiting the bugle call. Two walls are covered in bookshelves with familiar names; Scott, Longfellow, Tennyson. Faded eastern prayer mats cover the seats of Coromandel furniture arranged on an Afghan rug, the rich brown field woven with green palmettes and diagonal rows of hooped boteh.

Next to one of the windows is an antique Japanese screen. The panels are made of tight beige fabric with hundreds of colorful dots. As I get closer, I realize that each one of those dots is a fishing fly. Dozens of Dusty Millers, Black Rangers, and Silver Wilkinsons are arranged in star shaped patterns, their feathers still brightly colored, hooks still gleaming. Next to this screen is a small desk and on its surface, are tools for this hobby. Clumps of chenille and yarn, twists of colored feathers, and a magnifying glass are piled on the table next to an old reel and a battered tackle box.

Like the glass case containing the marble woman in the previous room, there is another case here. Under the glass is a collection of yellowed newspaper clippings, an official program of the 1924 Ascot races, and a black and white etching of a nude woman with flowers in her hair. In one corner of the case, a pair of old spectacles and an antique spyglass.

The room continues on to another room, filled almost to its entirely by a snooker table, immense with its curved wooden legs, white net pockets, and spotless expanse of green baize. An elaborate gas-lit snooker lamp hangs suspended from the ceiling. Four arms of slender gun metal grey pipes extend from the large metal flower which is the center, each arm ending in a bottle green globe. Ornate brass hooks hold several billiard cues against the wall and a wooden ball rack hangs next to a large slate scoreboard.

Instead of dark wood paneling, the walls are papered with black with gold and ivory fleur-de-lis. An old Burroughs and Watts record player sits in one corner of the room. I find the location of the cigar smell in a small wooden humidor next to the window. Using one finger, I ease the lid open to reveal four small cigars, perfectly arranged. There is a row of antique snuff boxes, some rectangular, some oblong, brown with green edging and gold leaf patterns and these too give off a faint smell of tobacco and age.

Turning back into the other room, I gasp at the wall opposite me. Although I had passed it when I first entered, I hadn't noticed what was suspended on the wall. I definitely notice now.

The wall is covered with ancient weaponry. Guns, swords, and bayonets cover its surface and I stand dumbfounded in front of it. Among the collection, I recognize a Scottish snaphaunce pistol, a fowling gun, a Blissett double barrel, a Saunders Queen Anne pistol, a crossbow, a Basket hilt broad sword, a flanged mace, and a claymore. There are more exotic types as well. A macahuitl with its thin obisidian blades, a curved kopis machete, a 15th century halberd. A strange looking weapon to my right catches my eye and upon further inspection, I realize that it is a sword, its edges covered with a row of sharks' teeth, which stick out from the thick blade like thorns from a rose.

I am edging to my right, standing on my tiptoes to peer at an antique cane blow gun mounted higher up on the wall when my elbow hits something on a stand next to me. It rattles on the stand and veers dangerously towards toppling off when I make a grab for it, righting it back so that it will not fall. When I realize what I have saved from crashing to the floor, I recoil with a small shriek of surprise.

It is a disembodied head. A sheep's head. Dusty glass eyes stare at me from its fuzzy skull, thick brown horns curving around to nearly touch the muzzle, the tips coated in silver. The hair on the ram's nose is patchy in places, some areas bald where the fine hairs have rubbed away with age. Where the neck should be, are four small brass wheels. There is a large peach-colored gemstone set in silver in the middle of the beast's forehead and it sparkles dully.

I am backing away from this macabre curiosity, rubbing my hands briskly on my trousers, when there is a noise from behind me. Still not completely recovered from the shock of the animal's head, I shriek again and whirl around. Colin is standing there and he too jumps as I scream. Looking around, he realizes what has made me jump and gives me a bemused look.

"What are you doing?"

"*What* is that?" I point to the head on the table.

"A snuff mull."

"In a sheep's *head*?"

"Ram's head, actually, but yeah. It was Laura's grandfather's. 18th century, or so he used to say."

I look at him, then back at the head, then back at Colin. Colin gives a small tired chuckle and goes over to the stand. He lifts the head slightly at an angle to reveal the wheels beneath.

"The wheels on the bottom are designed so that it can be pushed up and down the dinner table after the meal.

"On the *table?*"

"Yep.

I frown at it. "Where does the snuff go?"

Colin reaches forward and with a sharp click, moves the gemstone aside. Beneath the stone is a small silver-lined cavity. He pokes his finger inside.

"The snuff would go in here. Grandfather Sinclair used to bring it out as a joke, threatened to wheel it on the table. Laura's grandmother hated the thing. Wanted him to get rid of it. But he refused. Kept it in here." Colin gazes at the thing with a look of poignancy and gives a ghost of a smile.

I want to tell him how repulsed I am by it, but I bite my tongue. I am not going to ruin his brief moment of nostalgia.

"Laura would like if you would go upstairs and see her now." The moment of tender remembrance is gone and Colin's voice is once again tinged with weariness and defeat.

I nod in understanding. I explain I will need to go back to the study to fetch my notes and he follows me back through the house, sad and beaten like a lost puppy.

13

L aura is now in a wheelchair, the white shawl draped over her knees. There is more color to her face than there was this morning; the air alive with a frisson of confined energy.

"Hello, Carole. Tell me. What secrets have you revealed?"

"Well, so far I have managed to transpose three entries, although I have to tell you now, that unfortunately none of them mention a necklace." I pause, waiting for her disappointment. To my relief, it does not come as she waves her hand for me to continue.

"The very first entry in the diary is dated 1633. Jonet would have been 11 years old. It is a brief entry, discussing how she received the diary as a gift from her uncle.

I figured the necklace would have been something Jonet acquired as a grown woman, rather than a child. So I picked an entry later in the diary. It is dated autumn, 1645. The plague has hit Edinburgh."

"At this point, her mother has died." Laura interrupts me. I am impressed. Laura has done her homework.

"Exactly. Mary died in 1644, missing the plague by a year. It was brief, but devastating. Eleven times the plague came to

Edinburgh, but this was by far the worst. Over 1/3 of the city died. Ports were closed, people were left to fend for themselves. Jonet mentions that as they are far from the city, she believes they will be safe but she fears for her siblings and their families as they are still in the city and she has not heard from them. Although that is not surprising, because at this point, the city gates would have been shut and any correspondence would not have reached her."

"The third entry was taken closer to the first. As it turns out, it was written right after Jonet is married to Lord Sinclair, however there is no mention of a necklace or any possible betrothal gift. Her new husband lived outside of Edinburgh and traveled frequently back and forth to the city. Apparently he would bring Jonet gifts back from his travels. Plums, painted fans, and lemons. At the time, apparently sundials were all the rage. Lord Sinclair brought one back for Jonet to put in the garden."

"Does it mention what the sundial looked like?" Laura asks.

"No, it doesn't."

"How remarkable. We found a slate piece with Roman numerals among the boxes of Grandmother's things. Colin had said he thought it was part of an old sundial. It couldn't possibly be the same one, could it?"

I too am caught up in the fervor. I smile broadly at Laura.

"Come, we must find it. I must show it to you." Laura says. "Will you push the chair for me?"

"I, um, sure." My hands are clammy as I grasp the handles of the wheelchair. I take a deep breath and push. The chair lurches horrifically, throwing Laura to one side but does not move.

"Oh dear, Colin must have put the break on. It's the level next to the right wheel."

Face flaming with embarrassment, I unlatch the brake and turn the chair towards the door. The left wheel slams against the doorframe and the chair shudders at the impact.

I mumble my apologies, dismay in my voice.

"I have never pushed a wheelchair before."

"It's alright, you're doing fine." Laura's voice is reassuring, soothing but I am apprehensive to go any further.

Laura directs me towards a small door at the end of the hall. A latticed gate bars the entrance to an old elevator. I try my best not to jostle the chair and to squeeze us both in the confined space. The lift creaks, shudders, then begins the slow ascent. I assume this will take us up to the upper levels within the southern tower. My assumption is quickly confirmed.

Stepping out onto a large landing, I see there are only two rooms, one on either side. We turn into the room to the left and immediately I am overwhelmed. It is like someone has taken an entire wing of the National Museum and crammed it all into one room.

The room is shaped roughly hexagonal with small windows; a seat nestled in beneath each one. At Laura's instruction, I wheel her around the room and she begins to talk, explaining the artifacts and how her family obtained them. Every surface is littered with objects, the room with boxes, crates, and tables. I listen in silence, only half catching what she is saying as I am too distracted by the objects crowding the corners of the room.

The main piece is a tortoiseshell desk inlaid with brass which dominates one side of the room; Laura explains that it was made by Andre-Charles Bouelle, French cabinet maker at Versailles to Louis XIV in the early 18th century. Five tiny tea cups are stacked awkwardly one into each other on the surface of the desk, making a fragile tower of blue and white china, pink roses and gold leaf patterning. They are wedged in next to a broken fireplace bellows, the leather edges cracked and peeling. Next to one of the windows is an old pirate seat chest. Drawing back the lid, yards of crewel work bed hangings are crammed and piled on top of a Dutch Delft tobacco jar, its stepped brass dome cover perched above a styled scroll and flower cartouche. On the wall, a brass lantern clock with an engraved dial and pierced dolphin fret ticks faithfully next to a square mirror bordered by a dark, rich frame.

"Mahogany?" I ask, pointing to the mirror.

"Turtleshell." Laura giggles with delight. "Oh Carole, what a joy it is to have you here."

There are piles of Bristol Delft dishes, a rolled up Caucasian rug with its rust red field and ivory lozenge medallions, brass candlesticks from Scandinavia, even an old chamber pot which is now stuffed with dusty silk shawls, peacock feathers, and to my surprise, a cannonball. A mortar and pestle, a lobster tail helmet from the Netherlands, a single pigskin and galoon shoe, and a silver toddy ladle are in the next box. An elephant's tooth sits next to an ostrich egg on the window ledge.

At Laura's direction, I spend nearly an hour lifting boxes and sorting through crates, but we do not locate the slate dial. Suddenly inspiration hits.

"Dear me! I know exactly where I put it! How could I have forgotten? Come Carole, this way."

We head back out of the room, maneuvering around stacked paintings and sheet-covered containers. The room across the hall is more organized than the first, the furniture organized around a low table at the center of the room. The furniture is ornate, gold with plush crimson damask cushions and an ancient foot rest with faded pink fabric sits in front of an armchair next to the fire. The valences over the windows are wooden, carved into foliaceous arrangements and painted the same luxurious gold as the arm rests and legs of the furniture.

Laura points me towards a small secretarie with oyster walnut veneer, which folds down to form a writing desk with a secret compartment. At her instructions, I reveal the hidden compartment and pull out a small spice cabinet. There are 18 tiny drawers and pulling out several rewards me with a brief, phantom smell of the past. Clove, cinnamon, nutmeg and pepper fill the room in an invisible cloud. I set that aside and peer into the back of the recess. Sure enough, the slate piece was slotted in behind the cabinet.

"I totally forgot. I put it in there to prevent it from breaking. Seemed a safe place rather than stuffed in a box where it could be damaged."

In one corner of the room, I notice a tiny wooden door. It seems out of place.

"Where does this go?" I ask.

"To the top of the tower. Outside. Go ahead, go on up." Laura smiles at me.

I am reluctant to leave her here, even for a moment.

"Are you sure?"

"Of course my dear. I'll be fine. Do take care on the steps."

I pull at the iron handle and the door slides towards me with a creak of disuse. I have to duck to get through the doorway to avoid hitting my forehead on the low lintel. The air here is much colder and it is quite dark, the only light coming from the room behind me. The spiral staircase is extremely narrow, with slender, tapered steps and I keep one hand on each side of the wall as I cautiously make my way up. The light continues to fade as I move further away from Laura and then turning the corner, there is another door. Within the lock is a small key. It does not want budge so I wrench it violently to the right and with a rusty, gritty groan, the key turns and the door opens.

A sharp, biting wind takes my breath away. I gasp as my hair is whipped around my face and I pull my cardigan closer around my body to fight the chill. The door has exited onto a small landing and the curved crenellated wall at the edge keeps me from looking down from the edge of the tower. I stand, looking out, a 360 degree view of the landscape around the house.

There are no roads, no signs of people, only vast fields, occasionally dotted with sheep. The loch to the eastern side of the house is dull and flat, the wind causing the surface to look bleary and unfocused. The breeze is sharp in my ears and the tops of the trees bend to the onslaught of the wind. I stand here for several minutes, allowing myself a moment to clear my head, trying to think of nothing but the stark Scottish countryside. I am lost in thought and the sharp crack of a crow's call brings me back to reality. I have lost track of how long I have been up here and I remember Laura is waiting for me downstairs.

I head back through the door, trying to keep from falling down the stairs. Nearly reaching the bottom, there is the sound of music being played from the room below. Entering the room, I see Laura has managed to wheel herself over to where a small carved box sits on a low ledge. She looks up at me and beams, a proud parent to an achieving child.

"It's beautiful isn't it?"

I crouch down next to her. It is a music box, clearly several hundreds of years old.

"It's amazing." I breathe and allow myself to run my fingers gently over the surface. Laura is watching me and she too reaches out to caress the ancient piece.

"It's been in the family for centuries. I remember when I was little, I would have trouble sleeping. It would be wound and would play while I would fall asleep. How wonderful that it still plays after all these years." Her voice trails off and I realize suddenly how tired she has become.

I am about to mention to her that it is probably best if we go back downstairs but her voice stops me.

"Will you wind it for me?" Her voice is quiet, child-like.

I reach forward and

"I will take you back downstairs." I say after a moment. It is both a question and a statement.

"Yes, please."

We make our way back to the elevator and down to the floor below. We are both silent, lost to our own thoughts and inner demons.

14

I cannot sleep. I roll from one side of the large bed to the other in frustrated exhaustion. The sheets tangle around my bare legs and I punch at the pillow restlessly. The small clock by my bed reads just past one. Images are racing through my mind. I cannot lie here anymore. I fling back the blankets, shuffling my feet into a pair of slippers lying next to the bed. I retrieve the bathrobe from the back of the chair, pulling the belt ties snugly around my waist.

The door creaks slightly as I open it and peer out into the hall. The carpet runner extends only a few feet in either direction before being swallowed up by the yawning darkness. I grope for a light switch, my knuckles scraping painfully against the edge of a gilded frame before finally located a small button. Pressing it sends a flood of dim amber light down the corridor from the bronze sconces.

At the top of the staircase, I peer down. The steps are predominantly in shadow, but I slowly make my way down, holding tightly to the curving banister. The fountain to my left at the bottom of the stairs beckons to me from murky grey darkness, giving me the brief illusion of a disfigured man lurking, waiting. I jump slightly, my tired mind running wild.

I hurry into the kitchen, fueled by the sudden rush of fearful adrenaline to soothe my nerves and my sleeplessness with a cup of hot milky tea.

I carry the cup into the study. My notes are where I left them, in a fan-shaped paper flower next to the diary. I walk slowly around the room, both hands wrapped around the teacup, gaining warmth and solace from the heat. I stop before one of the large windows, wrapped against the cold by the thick velvet curtains.

The circular drive is in muted darkness, the fields and trees blending into a seamless swath of ebony night. The sky is full of stars. Living in Edinburgh with the myriad of city lights, I rarely see the stars, even on a clear night. This sky is so full, filled with clusters and patterns of tiny diamond shards and this endless beauty soothes me. I turn and go to leave.

Jonet's necklace pulses at me from the tattered illustration. It is in a protective plastic sheath and I run my fingers along the edge. I cannot help but marvel at the beauty of Jonet's drawing, admire the color, skill, and detailed care that has gone into its creation. Jonet's initials, in their elegant curls, sit at the corner of the page and this too I run my fingers over, musing, caressing.

I am out at the main entrance, ready to retire to my bed when the sound of music echoes faintly off of one of the side passages. I pause, one foot on the step, hand on the rail, and listen. It is piano music, soft, lilting, beautiful.

I push through the door into a shadowy corridor. Recalling my wandering earlier today, this passage extends to two sitting rooms and the billiard room. I remember the grand piano that gleaned from one of the sitting room corners. The music is slightly louder now, the gentle ebb and flow of Ludovico Einaudi's *Nuvole Bianche*, rising and falling like a soft wind.

I stop outside the sitting room. The door is nearly closed, except for a crease of light that spills out into the hallway. The music is haunting, hypnotic, and I lean again the wall to listen. Eyes closed, the music reaches out to me and pulls. It is so profoundly beautiful, my heart aches in its sadness. It slightly changes and then *Le Onde* mesmerizes me into a drowsy sense of contentment.

Peering through the crack, I am stunned. Sat at the piano is Colin, bent over the keys. Although his back is to me, I recognize what he is wearing. It is the military uniform from the wedding photo. Although my mind briefly questions, I shift slightly, knowing what I will see. Laura's wedding gown pools luxurious, like a mermaid's tail at the end of the chaise longue where she reclines. She is quiet, watching Colin play. Her eyes are half closed, shadows from the candelabra on the piano top flickering over her beautiful face. It is a breathtaking scene and I am suddenly filled with shame for secretly observing and fear of being caught intruding. I quickly turn and silently make my way back upstairs.

In my room, a slice of moonlight streams through, casting an opaque shaft of light over the bed. Leaving the curtains open, I sit on the bed and stare out at the crescent-shaped illumination. My mind is now blissfully clear and I sigh with a strange sense of contentment. I close my eyes, watching Colin play for his bride, Laura lying serenely, listening to the overwhelming intoxication of the piano. Small flashes of light gleam from the intricate beadwork on her dress and the smell of hot wax fill the room. I fall asleep, imagining I can hear the siren's call of *I Giorni* in the wind.

15

Today is my 25th birthday. William returned two days early from his trip to Edinburgh to surprise me. He is such a wonderful man! The ship, La Fleur, arrived several days ahead of schedule, thanks to a recent turn in the weather, and this permitted his early return. This morning, we celebrated with a glass of fine Burgundy and a sweet almond cake brought from the city. The coach was laden with wine and gifts. William brought me ebony handled brushes and a set of watercolors but my favorite present is a silver heart-shaped locket. It is so delicate, so intricately beautiful; my heart soars when I feel the blissfully cool heart against my skin.

Seeing it brought back a memory of long ago, before we were married, when I found that beautiful necklace on the High street. I had forgotten all about it! I can still recall its beauty, the clarity of the purple stone and the splendor of the gold as I held it up to sunlit window all those years ago. Perhaps it is still hidden away, concealed and…

Laura is distracted this morning. She is haggard and has lost the spark from the day before. She twists one of the daisies from the crystal vase around her skeletal fingers, the petals falling onto the shift in her lamp, blending in with the white fabric. I do not know what I should say, so I just sit, allowing her to think, to gather her thoughts. She is gazing out the window, a glazed look to her eyes. I make an attempt to bridge the stillness between us.

"I transcribed another entry last night." I cannot tell if she is actually listening, but I continue on.

"You will never believe, it actually mentions the necklace! The entry is dated May 1647, on the day of Jonet's 25th birthday. Her husband had arrived home early from Edinburgh and brought as a present a silver heart-shaped locket. She goes on by discussing how she remembers the amethyst necklace from so many years before." I shuffle the notes I have brought with me, nervously in my lap. "I should definitely be on the right track now."

There is a flutter of emotion in Laura's eyes, a soft twitch to her lips. The daisy has lost all of its petals, the stem a thin, sinewy rope in her hands.

"Life is a strange thing, isn't it Carole?"

I take a deep breath. "Yes, it is."

"The world can be so full of life, color, and warmth, and then so suddenly, without warning, everything starts to fade. Colors disappear, flowers die, the world succumbs to the darkness."

This is a dangerous conversation. The metaphors she is using will do nothing to lift her spirits, to fight the sickness in her body, but depress her and bring her further down. I struggle to find something to say.

"True, but the darkness can only last for so long." I offer.

It is meant as encouragement, to give her strength, hope that she will heal. There is a ghost, a glimmer of a smile at her lips. Then it is gone.

"Yes, only for so long." Laura echoes back at me. She finally pulls her gaze from the window.

16

The air is damp, heavy, and wet, the kind of cold that gets into your bones and takes a lengthy hot bath to shift. I tighten the coat around my middle, already feeling the icy fingers of chill shiver down my spine. I am desperately wishing for a hat and gloves; instead I turn the collar up around my neck and shove my hands deep into the pockets.

My meeting with Laura didn't last long. I didn't even have the chance to share anything further with her about the diary entry or the letter. Colin came in, bringing with him a tray of hot tea, took one look at Laura, and asked if I could come back later, that Laura needed to rest. I returned my notes to the study, and then decided I needed to get away, out of the house.

The door I have just come out of has led me onto the southernmost point of the grounds. The low stone wall, visible from my room, curves and meanders at the edge to my right. A rough, muddy path takes a wide arc away from the house, and then follows the edge of the stone on the eastern side. To my left, the house sits devoid of life and I cannot shake the ominous feeling which has settled over me. The windows in the house are like empty dead eyes and for a moment, I imagine a flicker of dark movement in one of the windows but at a second glance, there is nothing.

The sickly sweet, cloying smell of decay lingers; leaves fall from the trees and are forming soggy blankets beneath the trunks bordering the wall. There are lonely shafts of larkspur, still holding on to a few of their magenta and white-throated blossoms. To my left, in the middle of the grass, are rose bushes set into artistic patterns across the lawn and despite the rare pink bloom with browning petals, the stalks are skeletal, having long been stripped of their leaves. In the middle of this vanishing garden, there is a large fountain.

The grass squelches and slurps under my feet as I walk over to the marble sculpture. It towers into the grey sky with a wide circular pool at the bottom, a dry basin collecting dead leaves. An angel rises up from a curved scallop shell.

I sit on the low stone bench next to the fountain and huddle into my coat. I am frozen, my fingers numb, but I do not want to go back into the house. Ominous feelings press down on me and I feel claustrophobic.

Heading back along path, I find a small break in the wall, a section removed and the muddy path veers off to the right into the undergrowth. Immediately I find myself having to put my hands out on either side to maintain my balance as the path dips sharply downwards. Several times, I slip, my shoes making long grooves in the mud as I skid dangerously down the slope. The path is now dark, trees on either side pressing in, heavily overgrown with thistles, nettles, and bracken.

Finally, at the bottom, I stop to catch my breath and my footing. The path continues off to the right and across a small burn into a field. The loch is fully visible from here, a small flock of geese stand gawking at the water's edge. A small voice in my head tells me not to continue, to head back to the house, but a glimmer of grey stone to my left causes me to turn. Pushing through the branches lying low over the path, I find myself standing at the edge of a graveyard.

The entire plot is square-shaped, bordered by a sagging iron fence. Most of the grey stones are half-hidden, obscured by dead grass and weeds. There is a small gate at the entrance; it is open, but instinct tells me not to cross the threshold into this hallowed ground. There are several taller headstones, but the writing has faded and is obscured with black moss and I cannot read the names. Only one, a date of 1821, is clear but I cannot tell whether this marks the date of birth or death.

It is lonely, forbidden, and an unexplainable knot of fear gnaws away and gathers in my gut. A strong gust of wind rips through the trees and with a sharp crack, a large limb falls from the overhanging canopy and lands with a metallic clang across the gate, blocking the entrance. I have my sign. I scurry back to the house.

*   *   *

The strong hot spray of the shower rids my body of the chill but not the cold vise of uneasiness that now has me captive. I quickly dress and head down to the kitchen to make a pot of strong, black coffee. Time is running out.

I sit for several moments in the study, listening to the faithful tick of the grandfather clock. I have so far transcribed four entries, only the last alluding to the existence of the necklace. Jonet mentions the necklace, a memory from so long ago, and I know now that I need to go back in the diary, back several years to the beginning. Leafing carefully through the brittle pages, an entry near the front cover leaves me speechless. Although I have yet to read a word, I know that it is this entry which holds the information I need. I swear under my breath, wondering how on earth I had not thought to look for something like this before.

The pages of this entry are littered with images of the necklace. Both large and small drawings have been squeeze into the crease, along the edge, and at the bottom. A small heart has been lovingly added to the first line of the entry and even the crown has been drawn separately, with the three stones in life-like detail. Although these illustrations are black and white and slightly smeared, they dominate the page. I am getting close.

September 8, 1639

Today was the most exciting of days. I found a necklace on the Royal Mile and it is the most beautiful thing I have ever seen. Although I should endeavor to locate its owner, my desire to keep it is overwhelmingly strong and I have decided to hide it away where no one will find it. I have decided to put it in the most peculiar of places, somewhere no one would ever imagine...

Three and a half hours later, it is close to midnight. I have not seen Colin since early this morning when I met with Laura. The house has been eerily silent, and I lean back, exhausted, overwhelmed, ecstatic. The entry was dated May 8 1937, just before her sudden betrothal and marriage to Lord Sinclair. It discusses how she found the necklace, its beauty and design, and her decision to keep it, to hide it away. And in reading the final sentence of Jonet's entry, a flood of realization and disbelief hits me. I know exactly where Jonet's necklace is.

17

The clock next to my bed glares 4:12 am. After learning where the necklace is, I ran around the house like mad, trying to find Colin, to let him know of my discovery. But as before, the house was ominously quiet. I couldn't find him anywhere. Despite my adrenaline fuelled state, I slunk into bed at 2 and waited for sleep to come.

I am still lying here. I have tossed and turned, hundreds of thoughts and questions racing through my mind. I know where Jonet hid the necklace. I know there is a good chance it will still be there, hidden away nearly 400 years after its initial discovery on the High Street of Edinburgh.

Outside a storm had started to build. Like the soft applause of an appreciative audience, it gathered quietly, and then rapidly expanded to a roar, a swelling gust of sound. Now it was no longer was it tinkering off the window pane, but coming down like a waterfall, the pounding sound of endless waves.

I have never seen rain like this. I get up from bed and throw the window open wide. The water is bouncing up from the flagstones in the garden, coming down so hard and fast the air seems to be filled with a white mist. The rain pops against the house and staring out into the darkness, there is nothing but the rushing wind and the crackling endless rush of the deluge. I close the window and am turning back into bed when a shrieking sound, like air whistling sharply down the chimney rents the silence. It is a keening wail, animal-like, and the hair on my neck stands on end. The sound is horrific, a high-pitched knife-edge scream which goes on for several minutes without ceasing. It frightens me so severely that my teeth chatter and my blood runs cold. I hide under the blankets, putting my hands up to my ears to block out the sound, and squeeze my eyes shut, willing the silence to return.

*   *   *

I wake in a state of panic. The wake up from a deep sleep, heart pounding, panic. In my haste, I nearly fall out of bed onto the floor, the sheets tangled around my limbs. It is quarter to nine. I have been asleep for only about four hours. I dress quickly, throwing clothes on, hastily donning a bathrobe as I race down the stairs.

I need to find Colin, have him take me to Laura. Although Jonet's diary has revealed the location of the necklace, getting to it will not be entirely simple. There will be slight complications in actually locating it. We will need to make phone calls, return to Edinburgh, arrange for Laura to travel. My mind is on overdrive.

Calling out for Colin does not reward me with his presence. I race from room to room, down the corridors, but there is nothing but oppressive silence. The only indication of Colin's presence is a smashed whisky bottle on the kitchen floor, icy shards in a stagnant, brown puddle.

I find Colin in the drawing room, seated with his back to me at the piano. This time, the chaise longue is empty. He is bent over, leaning towards the music stand, as if studying one of the sheets of music.

"Colin! I've been looking everywhere for you. Jonet's necklace, I found it. Well, I mean, I know where it is! We are going to have to make some phone calls but if we could just..." Something in the way he moves causes me to fall silent.

His movements are jerky, erratic, like those of a marionette. His arms lift slightly then flop limply at his sides. A gargled, choking sound echoes from his throat. He slides to one end of the piano bench, pausing momentarily at the edge, as if steadying himself. He rises, but his back is still to me.

"Colin, are you alright? I can come back. We can talk later if you want, maybe with Laura because I think she will want to hear..."

At the mention of her name, his spine stiffens and his body jolts like hit with an electrical shock. An inhuman sound, low and keening, fills the room and slowly Colin turns. I find myself looking into the face of hell.

His face is swollen, unnaturally bloated, eyes yellowed, bloodshot slits. The stubble on his chin creates a menacing shadow across his jawline and he is breathing heavily, his lips flecked with saliva. The smell of vomit and whisky is pungent. He is in the same clothes as yesterday; they are heavily wrinkled and damp with sweat.

The vision before me freezes me in a state of paralyzed fear. I cannot move. Colin takes one step towards me.

"Too late." His voice is a venomous hiss. "TOO LATE." He stumbles slightly.

"Too late?" A tiny voice echoes. My voice sounds far away, foreign in my head.

"Laura is dead. *Dead.* Do you hear me?! Dead! DEAD!" He falls to his knees, the terrible scream I had heard the night before tearing out of his mouth.

The next thing I know, I am running. Running out of that room, down the corridor, away from that horrific sound and heart wrenching sight. Tears are streaming down my face, blurring my visions as I run, the bathrobe flapping behind me like a cape. I flee to the study, seeking refuge in that small space, and curl up into the forgiving arms of the large chair next to the fire.

Several hours later, I am awake, groggy and disoriented. I have cried myself to sleep, the strain of the last few days and the emotional exhaustion I have endured. My eyes are gritty and my cheeks are sticky with dried tears. I rub the sleeve of the robe across my face, a sickening weight on my heart.

Laura is dead. That beautiful, delicate woman is dead. And Colin was right. I had found Jonet's necklace but I was too late. Fresh tears spring to my eyes.

There is a cup of tea on the corner of the table next to my elbow. I stare at it, trying to figure out where it has come from. Colin must have brought it in while I was sleep. Although it is no longer steaming, the cup is still vaguely warm. The tea is lukewarm, acidic, overbrewed. I take another sip, grimacing over the metallic taste. Questions start to seep into my mind. What will happen now?

There is a noise from the doorway. Colin is standing there, arms at his sides, palms up, in a *forgive me* gesture, tears streaming down his face. His eyes plead with me silently and I open my mouth to say something, to tell him that I am sorry, but his face suddenly swims. I frown and blink but then there is nothing more.

18

There is a moment in everyone's life when the world of dreams and reality blurs.

There is a man standing over me. He is black and white, like an old television character. He is a mix of Santa Claus and Sherlock Holmes, dressed like a grandfatherly figure might with a soft wool cardigan, trousers, spectacles. His beard hangs grey and thin to the middle of his chest. There is a pipe in his teeth. Or perhaps it is a pencil. I open my mouth to speak to this dream man but no sound comes from my mouth. My head is stuffed with cotton, and my tongue is thick like a limp steak. This figure does not move, but perhaps frowns in the slightest. I sigh, turn back over and fall back to sleep.

*   *   *

About 30 miles away from the hospital, Colin stumbled, bruised, bleeding, and broken through the front door of Seton House. He felt as though his heart had been torn from his chest. He stumbled again, then fell with a crash onto the hard wood floor. He lay there, allowing both the emotional and physical pain to wash over him. He screamed, convulsed, shook with rage, agony, and loss. Finally, whimpering softly, he made his way through to the sitting room and pulled himself up on the couch. Tears soaked the cushions and blood seeped into his clothes.

He knew he shouldn't have driven the car but he wanted her gone. Gone from the nightmare his life had become. He wanted to be left with his grief and his broken heart. There was nothing else for him, no one left. Several hours of anguish passes and the sound of the clock on the mantel lulled him into a quiet, snuffling stupor. His gut ached, his body sore, his blood now dried and caked. His eyes were so swollen he could barely see out of them.

He sat up, a leaden feeling settling over his mind. He rubbed his hands over his face. He tried not to think of Laura. Tried not to think of the sound of her laughter. The vibrant color of her eyes. How beautiful she looked on their wedding day. He tried not to think of her lying upstairs on their bed, lying like a frozen angel.

There were things to do. He dragged himself to the shower and stripping off his clothes, sat down on the floor and once again, howled and sobbed with pain as needles of cold water froze his skin. Then to the kitchen to make a large pot of black coffee. There is now work to be done.

19

It is very white and I briefly think it might be because it is snowing. But it does not smell fresh and clean like snow. It smells clinical, industrial, *hospital-like*. This is definitely not a Scottish winter. A tube snakes out of my right arm and I frown at it, cocking my head to one side, trying to figure out what it is. A loud voice deepens my frown.

"Welcome back to us." It is a woman's voice, heavily Glaswegian. I crane my head slightly to the right and there is a tiny woman sitting on a stool next to me. She is tiny with dark hair cropped in a pixie cut, slightly pointed ears, and bright shiny eyes. I scowl at this elf woman, yet another dream figure to my mind. The woman chuckles and places the clipboard she is holding on the end of the bed.

"I'm Dr. McIntyre. You've created quite a mystery for us, my dear." She pulls the chair closer to the bed. "Do you know where you are?"

Although the realization was slowly dawning on me, I look around for effect. White room. Stark. Curtains closed to my left. Name tag reads Dr. McIntyre. Huh. So not an elf.

"Hospital." I croak. My voice is low, rumbly, grumpy. She beams at me like a child who has solved a difficult math problem.

"Can you tell me what your name is?" I tell her.

"Carole. With an e. Mathieson. With an e."

She frantically writes this down on the clipboard, repeating the spelling back to me.

"Can you tell me the last thing you remember?"

Yup, the 1950s television grandfather with the pipe. How he stood there and watched me as I slept. I tell her this. Her forehead creases momentarily then she puts her head back and laughs out loud. Dr. McIntyre leans forward, merriment in her eyes.

"That was Dr. Taylor. He was the emergency doctor on call yesterday when you arrived."

Yesterday? Huh. I have no idea what day it is. And despite a splitting headache, questions are forming in my head, but without any clarity. *What day was it? That man was not a grandfather? And how the hell did I end up in the hospital?*

I try to voice these concerns but speech fails me and my words are garbled and judging by the look on Dr. McIntyre's face, I am not making much sense. She lays a motherly hand on my arm and smiles gently.

"You were in a car accident sometime yesterday and were brought in during the early afternoon."

"I don't have a car."

"Can you tell me who you were in the car with?"

"I don't have a car."

I am getting agitated. I have no idea what she is talking about and my head is starting to pound. I raise my hand up to my head and there is something there. Soft and fuzzy. I pick at it and the doctor reaches out and pulls my hand away. That's when I notice a metal splint on two of the fingers on my left hand. Now that I think about it, it's not just my head that hurts. My hand is killing me. My chest hurts and my left leg is aching fiercely. My stomach is queasy and I try and think about the last time I ate. Nope. Nothing there. The doctor is peering intensely at me and I study her under lids half-closed by curiosity and pain.

Lab coat. Green sweater underneath. Silver thistle earrings. Crooked teeth. Eyes like a weasel's dark, shiny. They remind me of Colin's. Yes, exactly like Colin's when he first... *Colin.* This memory hits me like lightning and my body involuntarily lurches forward. I will learn later that this motion tears the IV port from my arm and scarlet drops of my blood land on the hem of the doctor's pristine white coat.

I start shouting, my arms waving wildly. "Colin! The car! OMG the car. And the damn tea cup!" I try and fling the blankets covering my knees from the bed and I flashback to Laura in her wheelchair, the thin linen covering her legs. I am panicking and my vision is starting to blur. I can hear some-one's voice yelling. It sounds like mine.

"Laura! No! Get the diary! *The goddamn diary!* Tell them in Edinburgh, tell them at the Close..."

*   *   *

When I wake up, I am in the same place as before. Same white room, same white bed. The television above my bed is off and the room is in shadow. I can hear the squeak of shoes somewhere nearby but other than that it is quiet. Slowly fragments of my encounter with Dr. McIntyre form in my mind. A sinking feeling settles in my stomach and I think of Laura, Colin, the Close. My heart aches. To my left however, there is a slight change. On the formerly empty windowsill, there is a riot of color. Several vases of orchids, daisies, sun-flowers, roses. A small teddy bear holding a shiny Mylar balloon. *Oh boy*. Things are definitely clearer now.

There is a tray near my elbow and it has a pitcher of ice water and a small cup with a pink straw. I try and reach for it but my movements are uncoordinated and clumsy and I knock it over. Water soaks the tray's paper liner.

I sigh heavily as tears prickle my eyes. I wait, letting them side down my cheeks, turning my face slightly and they quickly saturate the stiff pillowcase. I look from side to side, trying to locate the button among the sheets which will inevitably send a nurse to my bedside. Several seconds later, a busty redhead comes in with a smile on her face.

"You're awake." Her name tag reads Brenda. Her smile reveals rows of artificially whitened teeth. I think of Dr. McIntyre's crooked teeth.

"Is there something I can get for you?"

I don't say anything, just point to the water cup lying on its side. The cup is refilled and the straw is put in my mouth. I drain the glass and ask for another cup. The water is cold and feels oily on my tongue but is a salve to my cracked lips.

"I'm going to go and let the doctor know you are awake." Brenda bustles away.

About fifteen minutes pass before anyone comes back. I have lain there and tried to keep my mind occupied by count-ing the flowers in their vases. I refuse to think of anything else. Three vases. Four sunflowers. Seventeen roses, eleven yellow, two purple, four pink. Two pink orchids. And some sort of creeping vine. The bear is the color of toast with pink hearts for paws and a white heart nose. The balloon twists and turns and I am drowsy watching it. There are also twelve daises but I don't count them. I refuse to look at them.

The doctor comes in and it is not Dr. McIntyre or the first man from my dream world. He is in his 40s, darkly handsome and pulls up a seat alongside the bed. He holds his hand out to me.

"Hi there Carole, I'm Dr. Robert Merchiston. Dr. McIntyre's shift ended several hours ago and so I am now in charge of your care." I raise my right hand gingerly to awkwardly shake his hand. He smells of . I like him already.

"How are you feeling?"

"My head hurts."

"I'm not surprised. You have a severe concussion, a black eye, and a split lip."

"Could I have some drugs?" Mr. Handsome checks my chart, muses over it for a second, then winks at me.

"Hold tight, I'll be right back." While Handsome is gone, I investigate the damage to my face with my good hand. My lips are swollen like fat worms, cracked and leathery. None of my teeth are missing which is a relief but there is an alarming puffiness to my left cheek below my eye. Several minutes later, he is back with a vial of clear fluid which is put into my IV. A slow balm settles over me and the pain is replaced by a soothing sleepiness. My mind starts to cloud and I lay back, comfortable now, willing to let the drugs lull me into a drugged state. Handsome sits back down.

I turn my head towards him. Several seconds pass and I realize he is waiting for me to say something, anything.

"There was a car accident." I say and I realize now that the reason it had been so difficult to speak was because of my fat lower lip.

He nods. "Yes, you were a passenger in the vehicle. The car was driven off the road into a grove of trees and ended up crashing into a burn."

Goddamn it Colin. Drug my tea, put me in the car, and then crash the damn thing. Well done.

"Where's Colin?" I ask.

"Was Colin the driver?" Handsome is now taking notes. What did he mean, was Colin the driver? Of course he was. But if we had crashed, and I ended up in the hospital, where the hell was he?

"Yes. Is he not here?"

"You were the only person in the vehicle when it was discovered."

This causes me to lurch forward. Handsome has put his hands out to prevent me from accidentally tearing the IV from my hand again.

"Who found us?"

"A couple returning from a day trip to Loch Lomond. Saw the car's taillights in the bushes and stopped to phone the police."

I sit back and am silent at this. Colin wasn't in the car. But he had been driving. Had he wandered away? Was he hurt? Or lying somewhere, dead?

"The police have yet to locate him. They have searched the area."

If they had searched the area and not found his body, then Colin was alive. And I knew exactly where he would be.

20

The breeze ruffled the man's hair as he set the shovel down next to the pile of dark wet earth. It fell with a heavy thud. A large mass of daisies covered the mound at its head, the breeze scattering them from their disheveled pile. The man stood and stared down at the black soil caking his hands, tears making them slowly clean. Above him, the sky was streaked with grey and black clouds. A hawk circled overhead. Raindrops fell, mingling with the tears on his face. There were soft pattering noises as the drops of water fell on the freshly turned ground. Out on the loch, the wind whipped up whitecaps and a small boat quickly turned for land. There was a low rumble of thunder in the distance and the fast racing clouds had engulfed the Trossachs in a black mist like a shroud. The wind whistled through the trees and a flock of crows sat in a nearby oak's branches, buffeted from the wind, eyeing the man warily.

The man fell to his knees next to the grave. Water seeped into his trousers but he did not feel the cold. He did not feel anything. He was quivering; his breath was fast and erratic. A lone daisy was entwined between his fingers. His hands were shaking and the petals fell from the bloom, white satin against the black unforgiving earth. There was a pregnant silence, the air heavy and waiting. And then there was nothing but the sound of flapping wings as a single gunshot echoed over the water.

21

oday is my first day back at the Close. Although I won't be working, I have other plans. Back in 1639, days before her wedding, Jonet Nimmo hid her mysterious necklace in Mary King's Close. Although she would have never imagined the street she lived on and its myriad hiding places would someday become a well-known historic attraction, I am positive that if the necklace still exists it will be down in the bowels of the Close, hidden away in a niche in the stone walls. I am going back to search for Jonet's necklace. I phoned work last week to let them know I was ok. They had been contacted by the Hospital as they had no other contact details for me and in my wild ramblings, had apparently shouted continuously about Mary King's Close.

After being released from the hospital, I was interviewed by police countless times on what had happened. I didn't want to talk about it. My answers were brief and although this frustrated the investigating detective, he seemed to understand and took my clipped answers in stride. I just wanted to be left alone.

I leave home and make my way up the Grassmarket, onto Johnstone's Terrace, and plod my way along the Royal Mile.

The sky is blue above me and the sun is brilliantly bright, but it is not warm. There is a fresh cold breeze blowing in from the west and I tug my jacket lapels closer to my neck. There are few people on the streets this early in the morning, but I am comforted by the silence and the vacant streets. The Cathedral looks peaceful in the pale morning light and I stop to gaze at the glossy stained glass windows and crenelated spires. The weather vane at the top, the golden rooster, twirls softly.

Mary King's Close is not yet open. During our phone conversation, Owen suggested that I come in when the site was empty; there would be no customers or hoards of colleagues either desperate for a bit of gossip or sympathy for my ordeal. I agreed. I didn't want to deal with either.

Owen is waiting for me at the gate. He is a small, mousy man in his 50s with a comb over and spectacles. He tugs awkwardly at his orange and green striped cardigan which flaps in the wind as he holds the gate open with the grandeur of welcoming the queen. He was responsible for more than one of the floral vases which kept vigil at my hospital window. Owen steps forward, as if to embrace me, but catches himself.

"How are you Carole?" He peers into my face, nervous, expectant.

"I'm doing much better, thank you Owen. And for the flowers. They were beautiful."

Things are left at that and I follow him into the entrance to the Close. Sunlight streams through the windows and the old Burgh Courtroom is alive with dust and glazed light. After the cool breeze, the sunlight's warmth encases me in a cocoon and I momentarily shut my eyes and revel in the tepid embrace.

Owen is now standing with his hands in his pockets, shuffling from foot to foot.

"There won't be visitors in the site for nearly another two hours. Take as much time in the Close as you need."

There is no need for trivialities. I have already explained to him what I want to do and he was more than happy to allow me an unescorted wander through the Close.

I have learned that after my abduction, the site was shut down for several days while police combed the site and the glass was repaired over Stewart's Close.

*   *   *

The Close is cool, the air still and it is abnormally quiet. All of the sound recordings which enliven the Close during tours have yet to be switched on. I stand at the top, just off the stairs, the Close extending down the hill before me. The doorway into the laigh house is to my right but I won't be going anywhere but the main Close itself. If Jonet's necklace still exists, if it is still hidden along Mary King's Close, it will be in the main section. From the details in her diary, Jonet hid the necklace further down the Close from where her house was. But there is always a chance that I am completely wrong altogether. The section may have been demolished, or she may have hidden it somewhere else. I will not know unless I look.

The stone walls are heavy with the coating of white wash that was put in the Close during its use as an air raid shelter in WWII and I know that this will make finding the necklace even more difficult. Like finding the proverbial needle in a haystack. A 17th century haystack.

I move down the Close, my fingers brushing the stone, particles of the mortar falling to the ground. I make my way carefully down one side of the Close, then turn and climb back up again, running my hands over each stone and crevice. It is unlikely she would have hidden the necklace somewhere outside her range of height, as using a stool or any of the turnpike stairs in the dark would have drawn unwanted attention. This is what I am hoping. Time whisks by and I comb every inch of the walls. Nothing. With a sigh of defeat, I sit down on the ground at the top of the Close.

The lights in the Bowatt lamps flicker and dust filters through the beams of orange light. It is still silent. Strange relief floods me. I am glad I haven't found the necklace. The one person who had known of its existence and cared about it was now gone. With a lighter heart, I trudge back up the stairs to the gift shop.

As always, the lights in the shop make my eyes water and burn, having been accustomed to the dark for nearly an hour. It is now 9:15am. A half hour until the gates will open and a flood of tourists will stream through the door. Last minute preparations are being made to open the attraction. Feeling lost, I sit on one of the benches in the shop and watch my colleagues scurry around like bees at a hive. Banners are being hung, balloons are being inflated, shelves stocked and dusted, the large bell waxed to a dull shine.

Eilidh gives me an awkward, sympathetic smile, but says nothing and goes back to counting money for the till, avoiding my eyes.

Owen comes out and sits down on the bench next to me. Several minutes pass, and we sit watching the shop come to life.

"You doing alright?"

I smile and nod weakly.

"Any luck?"

"No." I whisper.

Owen sighs. "Maybe for the best."

I nod but say nothing.

"Can I get you something from the cafe, give you a few minutes?"

Gratefully I accept and follow him back to the manager's office. I sit in the large leather chair, brooding, staring out the window, seeing nothing. I am vaguely aware when Owen enters the room and leaves a steaming cup of tea in front of me, but I am lost in my thoughts and memories. I sit so long the tea turns cold.

There is a knock at the door and it swings inwards. Olivia, our duty supervisor, tentatively comes in, holding a large box. Her face shows confusion, wariness, and she smiles shyly. Few people at the Close have been privileged to know what I have been through; the rest has been left up to speculation and imagination.

"Hiya. I don't mean to interrupt but this just arrived. It has your name on it." Olivia shrugs at my questioning look. She is anxious to be away from the Close pariah and I watch her as she nervously sets the box on Owen's desk and flees the room.

I sit there and stare at the box. It is of medium size and a shot of fear trembles my insides. I reach for the tea, which is black and acrid and curdles my stomach. The box is addressed to Mary King's Close but my name is in large spidery lettering on the top. There is no return address, simply two words. Seton House. The coffee in my stomach flips and bile floods my throat as a cold sheen of sweat forms on my skin. When had this been sent? Prior to the accident? By Colin? By Laura?

Hands shaking, I search for a pair of scissors, using one of the blades to slit the tape running across the top. I gingerly lift one of the cardboard flaps with my finger. Nothing springs out at me. I take a deep breath to calm my racing heart and peer inside. I think I knew from the second I saw the words Seton House, I knew what must be inside. There are folds of shimmering pale green satin on the top. My Jonet costume. It is wrapped around something nestled in the bottom. A small casket. I lift it from the box.

It is rectangular, roughly 10 inches by six inches, with several plates of whalebone secured by metal straps on all four sides. Scalloped bronze plates covered each corner, each carved with an intricate, plaited design. The lid curves upwards and there is an old lock on the front.

On the top of the lid is a crisp white envelope, stiff in its newness. My name is written across the front, but in a different handwriting, this delicate, feminine, fluid. I turn it over and am surprised to see there is a tiny gold key suspended from an aged ribbon taped to the back. I gently pull the tape away from the envelope, turning the delicate key over in my hands before setting it down.

The envelope's seal breaks with a soft crackle and I pull out the folded letter.

Dearest Carole,

If you are reading this, then my time has come and we have not accomplished our goal. I am sorry. This life has been so short but blissfully sweet and I am truly glad that our paths crossed, despite the circumstances that they were. I cannot thank you enough for sharing your time here with us.

There is also good chance that Colin is gone as well. He

promised once that his love would follow me to the grave. Knowing his heart, I have no doubt Colin will have kept this promise.

With this letter, I leave to you the sole surviving pieces of Jonet Nimmo's life. I hope that you will share the pieces with others, let the world know her story. Jonet's necklace will remain forever lost. Perhaps it is the way it was always meant to be.

Love and farewell,

Laura Kinross

I fold the letter and clutch it to my chest. Tears run freely down my face.

The key slides gently into the casket and with a faint click, the lid opens.

On the top is Jonet's diary. Seeing it brings a rush of pain and memory and tears spring to my eyes as I lift it out.

At the bottom, there is more. A slightly tarnished Luckenbooth brooch. A gold band set with a glistening ruby. A lock of faded brown hair. A pressed daisy. And one of Jonet's watercolors of the necklace. These too I take from the box, almost reverently.

Although Jonet's necklace would never be found, Laura had provided me with a way for her legacy to be remembered. I would make sure no one would forget.

22

The gift shop is quieter than usual but today a new attraction has come to the Close. In one corner of the room, a small crowd gathers around a glass case. Under the freshly shined glass, a silver heart-shaped brooch sits next to a dried flower, a gold wedding ring, and a curl of brown hair. There are also pages from Jonet's letters and copies from the diary.

Tours are still running every fifteen minutes with full groups on each one. The glass has been repaired over Stewart's Close and to the first-time visitor to the site, they would not realize it had not been any other way.

Today there is a group of American students on the 13:15pm tour, on a three-week exchange program from the East Coast. They will be escorted by Ethan, one of the newly hired guides, who plays a plague cleaner called Walter King. They are noisy and excitable as they go around the site, having to be told numerous times to mind their head and their step.

The tour draws to a close and they follow Walter King back up to the staircase they came down at the beginning of the tour. One female student stumbles on the incline and puts a hand out to steady herself. Straightening, she wipes her hands on her jeans to rid them of the dust which has imprinted on her palms before continuing on, oblivious to the crumble of white plaster which detaches from the wall and falls to the ground.

Things resume in the underground world of Edinburgh. Tours continue, the electronic recordings echo down the street but now, in the air, there is the slightest change. As the golden light from the lanterns caroms across the stone walls, a sliver of amethyst winks in Mary King's Close.

ACKNOWLEDGEMENTS

This book would not have been possible without the two and a half years in the dark that provided me with inspiration, laughter, and the strangest Scottish accent you will ever hear. To my fellow Kingers, thank you.

Michael Harris – Thank you for being a sounding board in the early days of writing. Cheers to Schela 2008!

Krystiana Krupa – You were reading when you should have been writing. Thanks for getting this edited and ready to launch. *Fly Grasshopper Fly*.

Jayne Beebe – Thank you for the trips to the bookstore to spend my weekly $2 allowance. I wanted nothing else.

Joe Thomas – Thanks to you, I definitely know what a claymore is. Bring on the lobster creels…

To Auntie Bon – I'll never forget what you sent to me. It always gave me the motivation to make this happen. I wish you were able to read this.

Rob St. Clair – Thank you for introducing me to Seton House and for driving many miles down one lane roads in search of castles and ideas.

Duncan Lockerbie – Thank you for taking a chance on an overseas email and helping me make this a reality.

Edinburgh – For seven years, you were home. My real life fairy tale city.

My Scottish friends and family – A day doesn't go by when I don't think of you. Much love.

My American family (M, D, J, L, C) – No one on this earth believes in me like you do. I love you.

ABOUT THE AUTHOR

Dr. Jayne-Leigh Thomas worked at Mary King's Close for two and a half years, playing Jonet Nimmo while finishing her PhD in Archaeology from the University of Edinburgh. Many of the events in this story are based on true events or real locations within and around Mary King's Close and Edinburgh.

After living for 7 years in Scotland, she moved back to the United States where she works at Indiana University, directing a large archaeological and human rights project. Her second work of historical fiction is in progress.